A JOURNEY OF FAITH

A JOURNEY OF FAITH

KRISTIANA GREGORY

SCHOLASTIC INC.
New York Toronto London Auckland Sydney
Mexico City New Delhi Hong Kong Buenos Aires

No part of this publication may be reproduced in whole or in part, or stored in a retrieval system, or transmitted in any form or by any means, electronic, mechanical, photocopying, recording, or otherwise, without written permission of the publisher. For information regarding permission, write to Scholastic, Inc., Attention: Permissions Department, 557 Broadway, New York, NY 10012.

ISBN 0-439-43991-4

12 11 10 9 8 7 6 5 4 3 2   3 4 5 6 7 8/0
                                                      40

Printed in the U.S.A.
First printing, July 2003

Acknowledgments

I greatly appreciate the friendly advice, help, and re-source materials offered by George Elmore, Park Ranger/Historian, Fort Larned National Historic Site; and Dave Webb, Assistant Director, Kansas Heritage Center, Dodge City, Kansas. Their knowledge and enthusiasm for their state's history is awesome.

Thank you also to my crew of careful readers: friends Annie Anderson and MaryAnn Gould; my favorite duo Cody and Greg, the ones always searching for something in the fridge, and Kip, the one who fills it, but who is also my faithful sounding board; then especially to my intrepid editors, Kristin Earhart and Ann Reit.

And *gokki* to my research and travel companion, the best mom in the world, Jeanne Kern Gregory.

In Nomine Domini Nostri Jesu Christi

Table of Contents

CHAPTER ONE

───⟫◆⟪───

The Orphans

*N*essa Clemens reached in the corner for the chamber pot and carefully carried it through the hall and then down the servants' stairs. She had awoken later than usual and was now hurrying so she wouldn't get in trouble again. Mr. Carey would be angry and might accuse her of setting a bad example.

At thirteen, she was the eldest girl at the Missouri Orphans' Home. One of her many responsibilities was to clean the sleeping rooms each morning. Twelve girls upstairs shared one of these porcelain pots, and nine boys in the basement shared their own.

Though Nessa disliked this chore, she found herself smiling. Footsteps behind her meant five-year-old Mary was following her again, even though she was still supposed to be in bed. Mary had blue eyes and curly red hair that had come unbraided during the night and now fell over her shoulders like a shawl. She clung to Nessa's long skirt as they rounded the corner past the library, through another hallway, past the kitchen, and onto the back porch. Here Mary let go of Nessa's skirt to open the door for her, then when they were outside, resumed clinging to her for their short journey across the grassy yard to the privy.

The outhouse was a small, weathered building by the far fence. Mary opened its crooked door so Nessa could pour the contents through the hole in the seat.

It was spring. Red tulips and yellow tulips were blooming along the sunny side of the garden. Under the spreading branches of an oak tree was a pump and water bucket. When Nessa set the pot down to wash her hands, the child smiled up at her.

"You're a good girl, Mary," Nessa told her. "I needed your help today, thank you. But it's much too cold to be barefoot and you're not allowed to be outside this early. Come along, let's get you dressed properly so Mr. Carey won't punish you."

The sudden ringing of church bells drew her attention to the street. Yesterday was Palm Sunday, but why would bells be tolling on Monday? She looked over the fence and saw crowds of men cheering.

"The war's over!" came the cry.

Nessa grabbed Mary's hand and hurried to the front yard where they saw Miss Eva. She was carrying a basket of fresh rolls from the bakery.

"Oh, isn't it wonderful, Nessa!" she said. Miss Eva had red hair like Mary's, but hers was twisted ladylike atop her head for she was nineteen years old and served as their schoolteacher. They stood on the front porch, listening.

A newsboy with a brown sheet of paper in his hand was crying, "Extra, extra! General Lee surrenders his army! Extra!" He ran to Miss Eva when she waved him over.

She took two pennies from her purse to pay him. The ink was still shiny. Holding the newspaper along its edge so she wouldn't smudge the print, Miss Eva began reading aloud to the orphans now gathered on the porch.

"Boys and girls," she said, "this is the best news I've ever heard. The fighting is over. President Lincoln is a hero. He helped free the slaves and now he's helped bring our country peace. Finally, after five long years . . . oh, my . . ." Miss Eva choked back tears, but started to laugh when she saw their concerned faces.

"It's all right, children, I'm just so happy. Everyone is — look . . ." She pointed down the street. Board sidewalks ran the length of the block in front of stores that had tall, square fronts. Patriotic banners of red, white, and blue were being unfurled from rooftops — Nessa recognized them from last Fourth of July — and flags were planted in flower boxes. Church bells were still ringing, and people were pouring out of their homes and shops to embrace one another.

Miss Eva continued her impromptu lesson. "It's a day for celebration, children," she said. "The paper here says that throughout the states and territories, there'll be two-hundred-gun salutes at every army post. News is traveling by telegraph, pony, stagecoach, and ship. Soon, the whole world will know our Civil War is over. Maybe now my brother will be able to come home."

Nessa felt someone standing behind her. She turned to see Mr. Carey, the orphanage headmaster. From his vest pocket he pulled out his pocket watch. He opened it, stared for a long moment at the ticking hand, then closed the lid with a click.

"Miss Eva," he said, "it's half past eight. I gave you permission to visit the baker, not hold a political forum outside while school should be in session. As a result, you've lost your privilege of going to town for the rest of the week."

He looked at Nessa. She knew she must be polite, but she couldn't bring herself to meet his eyes. Instead, she gazed at the mole on his cheek and the untamed hairs growing from it. She wished Mr. Carey wasn't treating the end of the war as if it were any other day. She had liked seeing her teacher so happy, but now Miss Eva was just staring at the ground.

"As for you, Vanessa," he said, putting a heavy hand on her shoulder, "nothing to eat until supper. I've warned you not to let the children wander around in their night-clothes. Mary, you're to sit in the corner until noon. Run along now, all of you."

The classroom was upstairs. Light from an oil lamp cast shadows across their desks. Mr. Carey insisted the shades be pulled down so the students would not be distracted by the view and afternoon sunshine.

Nessa sat in the back row with Albert because they were the oldest. They had known each other since they were small, having both arrived at the orphanage within days of each other. He was taller than she was with brown eyes and a head of dark curls. He leaned back to search in his pocket, then handed her a small, cooked potato. Once again, he had smuggled something from breakfast. Mr. Carey often punished Nessa by making her go hungry, so Albert had long been sharing his food with her.

Grateful for his kindness, she smiled at him, then wrote on her slate, TOMORROW?

He nodded.

Tomorrow was his fourteenth birthday. He was going to live with the editor of the *Missouri Daily Gazette*. Mr. Carey had arranged for Albert to be apprenticed as a newsboy. Mr. Carey had a strict rule: Children must leave the orphanage when they turn fourteen.

Nessa erased her slate with her sleeve and wrote, I'M GLAD FOR YOU, then she looked away, feeling an ache in her throat.

Her fourteenth birthday was this Saturday.

Mr. Carey had arranged something for her, too.

CHAPTER TWO

———◆———

The Arrangement

Walking through town the next afternoon, Nessa passed clusters of men and women standing in front of shops, talking with one another about the end of the war. Every conversation she overheard was about the brave generals, or soldiers, or about a lost relative. At the post office, while Nessa was mailing a letter for Mr. Carey, two men were arguing about freed slaves moving west. It upset her to hear them say such terrible things about Negroes, so she hurried outside.

On her way home, she stopped at the newspaper office where several men stood on the sidewalk, waiting for the latest edition. Albert had been gone since only seven o'clock that morning, but she already missed him and wanted to say hello. Through the window, Nessa could see him setting tiny blocks of type into a frame, spelling out a headline. When she saw how hard he was concentrating on his new job she decided not to disturb him. She would try to return later.

In front of the Hotel Independence, a fiddler was

playing a hymn. Nessa stopped to listen. She knew it by heart. Several others gathered and began to sing, the men removing their hats to hold over their hearts.

> *What a Friend we have in Jesus,*
> *All our sins and griefs to bear!*
> *What a privilege to carry*
> *Ev'rything to God in prayer!*
> *O, what peace we often forfeit,*
> *O, what needless pain we bear,*
> *All because we do not carry*
> *Ev'rything to God in prayer.*

After several verses, the fiddler rested his bow and nodded to the appreciative crowd. Nessa didn't have any coins to drop in the cup by his feet, but she thanked him with a curtsy. The words to the hymn made her feel hopeful, yet she couldn't help remembering Mr. Carey's plan for her. The very thought of it filled her with dread.

When she rounded the corner by the orphanage, her heart sank and she realized she had lingered too long. Mr. Carey was waiting by the gate. His watch was in his palm, open. The silver lid caught the sunlight as he turned it toward her.

"Five minutes past noon. You should be ashamed of yourself — the only one who didn't show up on time for dinner." He pointed to a pail and scrub brush by the steps. "This should occupy you until supper, which, I'll remind you, will be at six sharp."

Nessa dipped the brush into the pail. After ten minutes, her hands were red from the hot water and lye. She felt humiliated to be out front on her knees, where passersby would see her. She wanted to cry. No matter how hard she tried to be good, Mr. Carey always seemed to be angry with her.

"Excuse me," a man said to Nessa as he escorted his wife up to the porch.

They stepped around the puddle she had made and smiled down at her. The woman was beautiful, with the same chestnut hair and blue eyes as Nessa's. Her heart leaped.

Maybe she's my mother, she thought, *or an aunt.* She often imagined this scenario when visitors came to look over the children. Maybe she had a family after all, who had been searching and searching and finally had found her. Or maybe a new family would want her.

But she knew this wouldn't happen. Mr. Carey had told her so.

"No one wants to adopt a child who constantly gets into trouble. Besides," he reminded her, "at the age of fourteen, I expect you orphans to make your own way in the world."

Albert was now at the newspaper and someday would be able to earn his living. And when Miss Eva had turned fourteen, she was offered the job as schoolteacher. Nessa wished she could be apprenticed as a cook or seamstress or journalist, but Mr. Carey had informed her he had a different surprise for her birthday.

"A new home," he had said, "a perfect situation."

Mr. Carey had arranged everything. It was a pleasant house surrounded by a picket fence and rosebushes. Reverend McDuff lived there with his three cats and a Negro cook. Next door was his church. It had stained-glass windows and a white steeple with a cross on top.

Nessa thought about the last time Mr. Carey had taken her there to visit. How her stomach had turned when she had realized she was to marry the minister! She'd known him since she was little, but never could she have imagined becoming his wife.

He was now in his thirties with wisps of hair combed over the top of his balding head, and a thin mustache. He was pleasant. In fact, he was often heard whistling as he walked through town. But Nessa felt uncomfortable being near him. His voice was so slow, he spoke as if he were about to yawn, which made her sleepy. And sitting through his sermons was excruciating. He rarely smiled or raised an eyebrow or showed any expression. Nessa thought his face looked like vanilla pudding.

During that visit, they had sat in the parlor on prickly red chairs, drinking tea the cook had served them. The room had been silent except for the grandfather clock. Its slow *tock . . . tock . . . tock . . . tock* had been torture for Nessa. Her cheeks had felt hot and she didn't know what to say. Finally, Reverend McDuff had leaned forward and took her hand. He looked at her with kind eyes.

"The Lord told me you're to be my bride," he had said. "I'll be good to you, dear, you'll see."

Nessa had been stunned. She had opened her mouth to respond, but then worried Mr. Carey would punish her for speaking her mind. After several moments of uncomfortable silence, she thanked the reverend for the tea and stood up to leave.

She had kept her thoughts to herself: *Why did God speak to Reverend McDuff about the marriage, but not to me?*

On their way home, Mr. Carey had said, "There's even better news for you, Nessa. The good reverend never wants to have children, so things'll be a lot easier on you. No children, no heartbreak."

Nessa had said nothing to Mr. Carey, but that night in bed she had cried silent tears. She loved children and had always wanted to become a mother. Another thing she knew for sure: As gentle and kind as the minister was, she did not love him.

She was still awake when the clock downstairs struck twelve midnight. Nessa got up and wrapped her blanket around her shoulders against the cold, for the rooms weren't heated. As she often did, she went to check on the babies and younger girls. Moonlight shone through the window and over the bare floor. At the crib with the ten-month-old twins, she rearranged the quilt they'd kicked off in their restlessness. At Mary's bed, she pulled the blanket up and tucked it in, then kissed her forehead. Nessa did this for the six others, too.

Standing in the doorway she whispered, "Dear Jesus, Miss Eva says we can bring all our worries to you, so here I am, asking You . . . please . . . oh, please show me what to do. . . . I'm so scared. . . . If I marry into a house where there's no hope of having children, I'll be even more lonely than I am now. . . ."

Then, gazing tenderly at the sleeping girls, Nessa continued, "And Lord, I pray these little ones will never be faced with a problem such as mine. . . . Please let them find true love."

CHAPTER THREE

Murder

The next morning, Nessa made her bed in the dark while everyone was still asleep. She was exhausted from having lain awake most of the night, tossing with anxiety. The dreaded day had arrived. Her fourteenth birthday.

She dropped her armload of firewood by the stove. A lantern on the table flickered as she brushed the woodchips from her apron and then hurried into the pantry. Breakfast was in two hours. Soon, the other children would be awake and beginning their chores. They would be hungry as wolves by the time they filed into the dining hall under Mr. Carey's watchful eye. He was proud of his hardworking orphans, but he always checked that they had first scrubbed their faces and hands before he would allow them to eat.

As the kitchen grew warm, Nessa poured oats into a kettle of boiling water. Mary had followed her downstairs and was sitting on the floor, cradling her doll. Nessa passed her fingers over the child's curly hair, then opened the window for fresh air. It was dark out. She was startled to see a light moving quickly up the street and to hear men shouting.

Something must be wrong. This was a lively town, but at this hour most people were asleep, not yet awakened by the backyard roosters. Through the stillness, she clearly heard the terrible words.

"Murder! Lincoln's been shot, the President is dead!"

Overwhelmed, Nessa slumped onto the bench. It couldn't be true.

As the light approached, she realized it was two men on horseback, carrying torches. Again and again they cried out to the darkened homes. "Murder!"

Mary looked at her with wide eyes. Nessa knew the child was distressed by the shouts, so she lifted her into her lap and rocked her.

"It's all right, Mary." She pressed her to her chest so the child would not see that she, too, was frightened.

Nessa didn't understand why, but now everything seemed horribly upside down. She sensed that nothing would ever be the same again.

At breakfast, before the children were allowed to butter their bread, Mr. Carey reported the shocking news: Far away, in the nation's capital, the President of the United States had been shot in the head while in a theater with his wife.

Most of the children were too young to understand what this meant, but Nessa felt a sharp grief. She remembered when she was four years old, being told that her father had been killed. Then someone had taken her for a long wagon ride through a forest and brought her to Independence, to the Missouri Children's Home. Ten years had passed and the orphanage was now the only memory she had of a home. Though she couldn't re-member the faces of her mother and father, she still car-ried an impression of them in her heart, which at times made her feel blue.

She felt ashamed for thinking of her own sorrow. She also was ashamed that in her mind she called Mr. Carey a windbag. He talked on and on. Couldn't he see how hungry the little ones were for their breakfast? He often did this, giving a speech that no one listened to.

Miss Eva had told Nessa that in earlier days, the orphan-age had been a mansion. It belonged to a harness maker who had prospered from all the travelers heading west on the Oregon Trail. Upon his death, the wealthy man had left his house and a substantial fortune to his nephew, Phinneas Horatio Carey — that is, Mr. Carey. For reasons unknown to most townspeople, Phinneas soon thereafter started taking in abandoned babies.

Nessa was curious about him. She wanted to know why someone who seemed irritated by children would want to be surrounded by them. He liked to read his newspaper to them after supper and give them candy at Christmas, but he was easily disappointed by the natural mistakes made by all youngsters.

"Everyone has a story," Miss Eva said, but this was all the teacher would tell her about Mr. Carey.

The back stairs of this mansion had been built for servants so the family and guests wouldn't have to see the untidiness of laundry and coal buckets being carried to the basement. But there were no longer any servants in the house. Tiptoeing down the narrow oak stairway from the attic, Nessa counted ten steps, then looked up. Above her was a stained-glass window. Sunlight filtered through, casting a patchwork of color across her apron.

Here was her favorite spot.

Nessa stretched her foot onto the banister and boosted herself up onto the wide sill that at one time held potted ferns. From her perch, she could look out a tiny oval of clear glass, above the treetops toward town. It was here she liked to come and think, her knees to her chest, her skirt tucked under her feet. Anyone walking upstairs or down would miss seeing her, especially if she sat as quietly as she was now. With all the other orphans in the house, this was the only place she could find for herself.

She thought about President Lincoln's murder as a light rain pattered against the window. *When he ate breakfast that Friday morning, if he had realized it was his last day, would he have done anything differently?*

Later that morning, as the familiar voices of the children reciting multiplication came from the classroom, Nessa stepped into the hall. She looked over the stairway, down to the parlor where Mr. Carey sat, reading a newspaper. It had been delivered moments earlier and was so freshly off the press, the ink had smudged his white shirtsleeves.

Lifting the hem of her skirt so she wouldn't trip, Nessa ran downstairs two steps at a time and was out the door with a slam.

She hurried down the street. A flag by the post office had been lowered to half-staff and there were black ribbons tied to a hitching post. The town's grief matched Nessa's. Miss Eva had dismissed her early from class because it was her birthday. Nessa wanted to feel happy about being another year older but instead felt miserable. By tomorrow, she must move out of the only home she'd ever known and into a new one.

As she walked around the block to avoid passing the minister's house, she had the same thought as before: *If God wanted me to marry Reverend McDuff, wouldn't He have spoken to my heart?*

The question still troubled her. She felt sick to her stomach wondering what to do, wondering what *God* wanted her to do.

She turned a corner and headed for the center of town. The street was noisy with wagons and the splashes of mud as their wheels rolled through puddles. Newsboys shouted the latest headlines that arrived regularly by telegraph. Shopkeepers framed their doors and windows with black cloth and then stood outside to talk with friends. Many shared a newspaper, reading together the tragic story. A murdered president, shot on Good Friday no less.

They shook their heads in disbelief.

Men discussed how they wanted to help catch the killer, an actor by the name of John Wilkes Booth. Never mind the $10,000 reward. They would do it for nothing. To make matters worse, on the same evening, Secretary of State Seward and his son were stabbed by one of Booth's accomplices.

Just six days earlier, there had been celebrations. Now this. Once again, people were all talking about the same thing.

Church bells tolled in slow, mournful peals. It was April 15, 1865, a day none of them would ever forget.

CHAPTER FOUR

A Young Bride

Nessa peered in the window of the newspaper office. She could see Albert working over the printing press. When he saw her waving to him, he came outside, wiping his inky hands on a rag.

"Mornin', Nessa." He blushed when he smiled at her. She noticed he reached toward her, but he quickly pulled back at the sight of his stained fingers. Instead, he put his hands in his pockets. A black apron covered the front of his clothes. She guessed from the bits of straw in his curls that Albert had slept in the barn.

"It's your birthday, ain't it?"

She nodded.

"I reckon you still have to marry the preacher tomorrow . . . yes?"

Nessa looked past him and caught her reflection in the window. She saw a girl with reddish-brown hair braided over her shoulders, blue ribbons on the ends. Her dress was blue gingham — faded from so many washings — with white buttons up to her collar and along her sleeves. A ruffle from her petticoat showed beneath her hem. It came to the tops of her high-buttoned shoes, which were scuffed from the orphans who had worn them before her. She wished her dress fit her better and was longer, covering her ankles like other girls'. And she wished the tears that pooled in her eyes right now would stop.

After a moment she said, "If only I could work here with you, Albert." She wanted to be near him, like at the orphanage, but she also knew she needed to earn money to make a life of her own.

Nessa now remembered that a few months ago she had learned about a small sum of money saved for her for the past ten years. It was a mysterious gift from the stranger who brought her to the orphanage in the night. The money was in Mr. Carey's safe. It was hers, but he was not going to give it to her until she married Reverend McDuff. She didn't understand why. Whenever she tried asking about the matter, Mr. Carey grew angry and threatened to make her leave the orphanage early. She would have to live as someone's servant if she didn't do what he said. Nessa was even more discouraged when he explained how few people were willing to hire orphans.

"No one trusts 'em," he had said.

The sidewalk where Nessa and Albert stood resembled a narrow wooden bridge. It jolted from the heavy footsteps of passersby. Poplars and cottonwood trees cast spindly shade from their bare limbs. Across the muddy street, a blacksmith worked over an anvil with his apprentice. Next to his workshop was a large corral. It was here that mules and horses, and sometimes oxen, rested while their owners waited for wagon repairs. Some men were unharnessing a team from a stagecoach and leading the horses to water.

Albert nodded toward the coach. "They won't be leavin' till tomorrow," he said. "One of the drivers got kilt by Comanches and the other one quit, so they're lookin' for a new fella to take the reins."

"*Killed?* Why? How do you know so much, anyway?"

He pointed behind him to the sign stenciled along the top of the window: MISSOURI DAILY GAZETTE. "We hear all the news, whether it's true or not," he said.

A chill breeze rattled the branches overhead. Nessa stepped out of the shade into the sun to get warm. Still looking across the street, she asked, "Where's the next stage going?"

"West, into Kansas," said Albert, "to Fort Larned. The army's there to protect the trail. This coach'll be deliverin' mail and some military wives, I hear."

Nessa turned to face him. "What else is out there?" she asked.

"Nothin' . . . just prairie and Indians. And the town there."

"What town?" She raised her eyebrows with interest.

Albert sighed. "Nessa, I got a bad feelin' you're gonna get into trouble again. You wouldn't like it out there. The town is little — so little it's barely a dot on a map."

Last year she had run away when one of the younger girls was adopted. Nessa had convinced herself that the family would want her, too, so she followed their carriage to the harbor. She was caught boarding a riverboat, heading south. That evening, Mr. Carey had whipped her in front of the other orphans as a lesson. Albert had begged her never to run away again.

Now to discourage her, he began repeating every dreadful, horrible thing he'd heard about this town called Prairie River. It was part of Fort Larned on the Santa Fe Trail and would take days to get there. Kiowa and Cheyenne war parties often ambushed travelers. Outlaws ran free because there were no lawmen, and the soldiers were too busy with the Indians, trying to keep the peace. Besides, there were rattlesnakes and bobcats. Wolves. Tornados.

And with President Lincoln dead, who knew what might happen to the country?

But the more he told her, the more Nessa's face lit up.

"Albert, d'you reckon the town might have families with mothers and fathers and children?"

At this, he threw his hands in the air.

"You can't go there, Nessa, you just can't. It's millions of miles from nowhere, it's dangerous, it's . . ." His words trailed off. He looked into her blue eyes and gently shook his head.

An unfamiliar silence fell between the two friends as they stood in the sunshine watching the crowd. Two ladies strolled by wearing black shawls for mourning. Their dresses rustled with their steps.

". . . and Mrs. Lincoln's gown was covered with blood . . ." one of them was saying. "She and the president were holding hands like sweethearts the moment he was shot. . . ."

This reminded Nessa that she was probably the only person not thinking about the nation's tragedy today. She wished she could pay attention to the news, but tomorrow she must be the bride of an older man she hardly knew, a man who did not want to have a family.

She felt cold and sick inside.

"Albert?" Nessa asked, looking down at her boots. "Do you think God truly said I'm supposed to marry Reverend McDuff?"

A sudden tapping at the window drew their attention to the editor's angry face. Albert gave Nessa a good-bye glance and hurried into the building.

Just before she turned away, she saw her friend through the glass door, looking out at her. Albert was shaking his head and mouthing the words, "Don't . . . marry . . . him!"

Nessa felt a lump in her throat when he pressed his hand to the glass. She hurried forward and did the same, their palms and fingers perfectly matched. If the glass hadn't separated them, she was sure she would have clung to him.

After supper, Nessa sat on the end of her bed, staring at the valise she had packed. Tomorrow was her wedding day. She had only a few things that she could call her own: an extra petticoat and drawers, a shawl, an apron, a pair of stockings, her Bible — it was bound in red leather and small enough to fit in her hand. She took it out, wanting to read something that would comfort her, but the pages looked blurry. Instead, she closed her eyes and listened to the voices of the other girls.

Eight of them shared this cold room. All were in their nightgowns, brushing out their braids. They ranged in age from seven to twelve; the infants and younger ones such as Mary were in the room next door, the boys were downstairs. How she would miss everyone! In her mind she said each one of their names, asking God to watch over them. She couldn't think about Mr. Carey without feeling mean.

It was Nessa's last night here. She did not want to sleep, and she did not want tomorrow to come. Silently, she prayed, *Dear Jesus, please comfort Mr. Lincoln's wife and give her strength . . . give both of us courage to face tomorrow . . . please.*

Wrapping herself in her blanket, she climbed the dark stairway to the attic, where there was a room at the end of the hall. She knocked softly. From inside came the sound of footsteps, then Miss Eva opened the door, holding up a candle to see who was there.

"Nessa, do come in." Miss Eva's red hair hung to her waist. In the candlelight she looked delicate and beautiful.

"Miss Eva, I've come to ask you a favor."

There was so much Nessa wanted to say, but didn't know where to start. Instead, tears came. Miss Eva set the candle on the windowsill and pulled Nessa into her arms. Ever since the whipping last year, she had tenderly cared for Nessa as if they were sisters.

After some moments, Nessa wiped her cheeks with the back of her hand and began to explain her plan.

CHAPTER FIVE

———◆◇◆———

The Money Pouch

After a sleepness night, Nessa crept downstairs with her bag just before sunrise. She let herself out of the house, quietly closing the door. The air was cold and the black sky brimmed with stars. She could see the kitchen where lamplight cast a yellow square onto the dirt outside. Through the curtain she saw the slender silhouette of Miss Eva at the stove.

When Nessa came to Reverend McDuff's house, she opened the gate. From her bag she took the letter she'd written last night, tiptoed up to the porch, and slipped it under the door. As she turned to leave, she noticed one white corner of the envelope. She hesitated. It wasn't too late to pull the letter back, to change her mind.

Is it a sin to run away from a betrothal? she wondered.

Suddenly, she saw candlelight flicker from inside the parlor, and there was a shuffle of shoes along the wood floor.

In a panic, she hurried down the steps and ran to the depot, afraid to look behind her. Lifting her skirts so she wouldn't trip, she rounded the corner of the blacksmith's corral. Torches made an oasis of light on the dark street. The stagecoach she'd seen yesterday was there with a team of six horses. Their breath made steam in the air. A man threw a mail sack onto its roof, wedging it among some trunks. Nessa slowed to a walk, trying to look confident. She noticed two well-dressed women in hoopskirts with gloves and bonnets.

Inside the station, a man at the ticket window called out, "Five minutes till boarding . . . five minutes!"

Nessa rushed to the counter. Trying to catch her breath, she said, "Prairie River, please."

The man looked at her over the tops of his glasses. "Thirty-one dollars and fifty cents," he said.

From her sleeve she took out a handkerchief that had been sewn to make a little purse. Here was where her money was hidden. When she pulled out fifty dollars and began counting, he snatched the bills from her fingers.

Without looking at her he said, "Ain't none of my beeswax, young lady, but does Mr. Carey know you're here?" He stamped her ticket with one hard blow, as if hammering a nail. Nessa didn't answer. She held her breath, waiting for him to question her further, but he slammed the window shut and pulled down a shade with the word CLOSED painted on it. He hadn't given her any change. She was embarrassed to ask for it and was in too much of a hurry.

Outside, she looked toward the orphanage. An upstairs room glowed with light. When someone pulled aside a curtain to look out, Nessa dashed into the coach, hoping she hadn't been seen. The ladies were already inside, chattering and arranging their voluminous skirts. Nessa sat opposite them, on the bench facing forward. She gave them a quick smile, but turned her gaze to the window. Her stomach was upset and she was worried about getting caught again.

Had Mr. Carey heard her leave? Was he coming after her? Her heart raced now knowing that he and the ticket man were acquaintances — was he going to report her? And what if Reverend McDuff found her letter — he, too, might come looking.

Please hurry, she thought, *hurry,* as the driver pulled himself up to his roof seat. She could hear his boots scrape overhead as he settled in. She wondered what was taking so long. Finally, the driver gave a shout and snapped the reins. To her relief, the coach jolted forward. Nessa managed to grab one of the straps hanging from the ceiling, but the ladies slid to the floor. She momentarily forgot her nervousness and bent down to help them.

By the time they had introduced themselves, the coach was on the edge of the sleeping town, heading southwest along the Santa Fe Trail. Fanny Jo and Laura were sisters, and one of them was married to a lieutenant assigned to Fort Larned. They would be living comfortably in the officers' quarters. Nessa revealed only that she was going to Prairie River. When asked why she was traveling alone and where her family was, her mind raced with what she should say. She wanted to be cordial, but was too nervous to think straight.

Finally, she answered, "I prefer not to say at present."

There was an awkward silence.

"Well, I declare," said Fanny Jo, "just look at this mess." The floor was littered with the dark shapes of cosmetics and other such items that had spilled from their valises. As they began gathering their things, Nessa leaned through the window to look out. The road behind them was dark except for a prick of light in the distance. She couldn't tell if it was from a house or if someone was riding with a lantern.

She sank back into her seat, feeling desperate. She didn't want it to be like the last time she tried to escape. She had been so close. The riverboat captain had just pulled the whistle, the paddles were beginning to churn the water, when shouts from shore had made everyone stop. Nessa had been hiding in an apple barrel until a boy opened the lid and pointed to her. She had been furious at herself for having told him earlier she was running away. Mr. Carey had rewarded him with a silver dollar and a pat on the head.

Nessa was not going to make that mistake again, trusting strangers.

By sunrise, no one had caught up to them. The swaying of the coach began to feel comfortable, and Nessa turned her thoughts to Reverend McDuff. Surely, he would have read her letter by now. Their marriage ceremony was to have taken place that evening, officiated by a minister from another town. She didn't know how to disagree with a preacher, or if she was even allowed to, so she merely wrote, "Thank you, anyway, kind sir, but I am not going to marry you." It was Easter Sunday. Maybe at this moment he was walking to church to give his sermon.

Again she was overcome by a terrible thought. *What if God has spoken and said I should marry the reverend, but I wasn't listening? Would that be a sin?*

As Nessa fretted over this, she watched the Missouri woodlands pass swiftly by and turn lighter shades of green as the sun rose in the sky. Whenever the coach turned into a curve, she could see the strong horses and the dirt thrown up by their hooves. Dust covered her dress and stung her eyes. Whether they had done so intentionally or not, the sisters had taken the better seat, facing backward out of the wind.

Nessa remembered last night when she and Miss Eva sneaked into Mr. Carey's office. By the light of their candle, they found the combination to his safe written inside his ledger. After twisting the dial this way and that, it clicked open and they retrieved a leather pouch with a tag attached to it: NESSA CLEMENS, 1855.

The year had been 1855 when she arrived at the orphanage.

For the next hour, they sat on the floor of Miss Eva's room. They tore pieces of stationery into the exact size of currency. With a penknife, they cut the copper buttons from Miss Eva's coat to match the smaller coins. The silver half-dollars they replaced with heavy brass knobs unscrewed from her cabinet doors. When done, they weighed in their hands the pile of money against the trinkets, then filled the pouch.

"Miss Eva, will you get in trouble for this? Are we stealing?"

"Not at all, dear. Every cent belongs to you. Besides, you'll be long gone before Mr. Carey discovers the switch. Don't worry about me." All counted, there were fifty-six dollars, more money than either of them had ever seen. Then Miss Eva gave her twenty dollars of her own savings. "You may need this," she had said.

Nessa stared out at the countryside and blinked fast to keep from crying. Miss Eva had been her teacher and a true friend. She missed her already.

Every fifteen or twenty miles, the coach pulled to the side of the trail where there was a stage stop, to water the horses. The sisters and Nessa were invited to drink from a common bucket and use a privy behind the house. She was grateful for the biscuits and salt pork Miss Eva had packed, for by noon she was famished.

And though she knew it was unladylike, Nessa marched around the corral, swinging her arms to stretch out her stiff muscles. It felt wonderful to be out of the coach with all its wind and dust, even if for just a few minutes.

During one of these stops, a boy helping with the horses reminded her so much of Albert she almost called his name. Only then did she realize the letter she'd written her friend was still in her bag. She'd been so unnerved by the light in the minister's house, and in such a hurry to escape town, she'd forgotten to slide it under the door of the newspaper office.

She was heartsick. Now Albert would wonder where she was and worry about her. He might think she had left town without a thought of him.

CHAPTER SIX

A New Passenger

After they crossed the Missouri border into Kansas, the lush fields faded behind them. The land was now flat, a pale green from new grass. Along the way, they passed groups of covered wagons slowly traveling together to Oregon. In many places, they were spread out across the trail to avoid one another's dust. The sight of children walking alongside the wagons made Nessa smile. She felt happy thinking these families were traveling together.

Late each afternoon before sunset, the coach stopped at an inn where black cloth hung from windows. It seemed everyone across the land was mourning President Lincoln.

Nessa wondered what she would have done without Miss Eva's twenty dollars. Supper cost twenty-five cents, so did breakfast. She paid fifty cents to share a bed with the sisters, and though comforted by their presence, she couldn't sleep. The scene with the ticket man kept playing in her mind and made her angry. She wished she'd been brave enough to demand her change.

Before starting out on the fourth morning, the driver

put on his leather gloves and took the reins. He sat high up on his seat, talking to the innkeeper, who was tying down another trunk to the roof.

Nessa strained to listen. She heard the words *ambushed* and *fierce*, and remembered the previous driver had been killed. She knew there was a rifle up top.

A new passenger sat beside her. Mr. Button was a large man with a mustache that curled up his cheeks like wings. He settled into the coach as if he owned it, spreading himself over half the seat with newspapers and books. From his pocket, he took out a pair of spectacles and put them on, hooking the wire rims over each ear.

"Indians," he said, offering an explanation of the discussion taking place outside. "They're all over the place and mad as hornets that white folks are settling their land."

The sisters and Nessa exchanged looks of worry. Over the past days they had become friendly, though Nessa told them nothing about the orphanage. She learned they were from Pennsylvania and had been staying in Independence until they could find a coach heading west.

She also learned that their cheerfulness hid a great sorrow: One of their brothers had been killed during the Battle of Gettysburg; another had starved to death in Andersonville prison. When Fanny Jo received a letter from her husband saying his company would be at Fort Larned, they decided to come surprise him.

The younger sister, Laura, said, "But the trail is safe, yes? We were told that soldiers will escort us if there's danger."

Mr. Button sighed so heavily his mustache fluttered. "Of *course* they say that. Otherwise no one would want to settle this new state." His stomach bulged beneath his shirt, straining the seams of his vest. He spread his feet apart so he could bend over to look in his valise. When he sat up, he was out of breath from the effort but smiling. He held up a bag of candy and offered it around. As Nessa reached her hand inside, she realized the bag was actually one of the man's socks, mended in the toes and heel.

The sisters politely refused, but Nessa had already taken a piece. There was a wonderful scent of cinnamon and peppermint — how she wanted to eat it! She hadn't tasted candy since Christmas. The thought of the man's foot having been in the sock was unpleasant, but not horrible. She didn't want to hurt his feelings, and so, thanking him, she put the candy in her cheek. It was deliciously sweet.

Mr. Button pointed out the window to where the Oregon Trail branched off from theirs, heading northwest. In the distance was a line of dust following what looked like small white sails.

"Lookee there," he said. "More prairie schooners. Reckon it'll take 'em months to get over the mountains and hopefully before snow sets in. I wonder if they've heard the news about our poor president."

As the miles swept by, there were fewer trees. Tall, waving grass spread to the horizon with wildflowers, like patched quilts of red, blue, and gold. An occasional curl of smoke indicated a homestead, its roof barely visible from the bottomland. Wind coming into the coach smelled of clover and dust from the road.

They continually passed slow-moving freight wagons pulled by oxen. When they met traffic coming from the other direction, the stagecoach veered off the road to make room for them. The sound of brush sweeping under the carriage always alerted Nessa to grab a hanging strap to keep from being bumped off her seat.

Mr. Button leaned into his corner and was soon dozing. His mouth dropped open. Fanny Jo and Laura talked between themselves. Seeing the way their heads touched as they whispered made Nessa wish she had a sister. She wished Miss Eva were here so she could confide what was now troubling her.

In her desperation to leave she hadn't thought about what she'd do once she arrived in Prairie River. She wouldn't know a soul there. Nessa watched the vast countryside. Each hour took them farther and farther from civilization. Albert had warned her about the dangers, but at the time they seemed more like stories, not something real. Fear was growing inside her. Where would she live? How would she earn her keep? She never again wanted to sleep in a cold bed without enough covers, but now she might have no bed at all.

The wheels of the coach rumbled over a rough stretch of trail, vibrating the floor. Her valise slid away from her, resting against Mr. Button's outstretched legs. Suddenly, she remembered the note Miss Eva had given her the night they said farewell.

Nessa found the envelope inside her Bible. With her fingernail, she broke open the wax seal.

Dear Nessa,
The same God in Heaven who watched over you at this orphanage will watch over you in Prairie River. As Proverbs 3 says, "Trust in the Lord with all thine heart and lean not unto thine own understanding. In all thy ways acknowledge Him, and He shall direct thy paths."
Miss Eva

Sighing, Nessa closed her eyes. Miss Eva's words soothed her as if she had drunk a cup of warm milk.

Rolling prairie gave way to willows and cottonwoods lining the Neosho River. Nessa could smell the water and feel the horses slow to a trot. They would camp here for the night along with other travelers. The town of Council Grove was here, with several trading posts and blacksmiths along the dusty main street. Even this remote place had draped its window ledges in black.

The driver climbed down from his seat and began undoing harnesses. "If you need provisions, yonder is the place to go." He nodded toward a small stone building in the shadow of an oak tree. A sign out front said LAST CHANCE STORE.

"Ain't gonna be no other place to buy nothin'," he said, "till we get to Fort Zarah, but it's days away from here."

Nessa stepped inside to a wondrous display of items

she'd never before seen. A buffalo head hung near the door. A stuffed bobcat and panther crouched on a top shelf as if ready to leap. There were deerskin shirts and moccasins, knives in leather sheaths, a two-foot-tall drum, a tomahawk, and a war club. Shelves along a wall held bolts of cloth, canned fruit and oysters, hammers, cooking pots, candles, wire, and oil lamps. On the floor were barrels of pickles, sauerkraut, sugar, flour, and beans. Nessa unfolded a blanket from a stack that was on a table.

"How much, sir?" she asked a man behind the counter.

"Five dollars." He leaned over a bucket to spit. "But if you wanna stay warm, this here's your best bet." From a shelf, he took down a bundle of fur, unrolled it, and then spread it out on the dirt floor. Dust puffed up around its edges. It was dark brown and shaggy with an odor of musk. As she knelt to run her fingers through the fur, he said, "Buff'lo. Shot 'er myself. Ten dollars, young lady, and you will thank me come December."

Nessa thought about the drafty orphanage where last winter she had trouble sleeping because of the cold. The other girls were allowed to sleep together in twos and threes to stay warm, but Mr. Carey didn't want her to be spoiled. He said this way she would appreciate being married and sharing a bed with Reverend McDuff.

"I have ten dollars," she told the trader. It seemed a fair price, though she had never purchased anything like this. She was willing to buy the warmth Mr. Carey had denied her.

A wooden mailbox against a wall reminded her of Albert. When the man said postage to Independence was five dollars, on account of them being so isolated, Nessa figured in her head what she already spent: fifty dollars for her ticket, three dollars for lodging and meals, and now the buffalo robe. Another four dollars for jerky, hardtack, and dried apricots to last the rest of her journey.

That left nine dollars. She would have to wait to mail Albert's letter.

After she paid the man, he rolled up the buffalo robe and put it in her arms. It was so heavy it pinned her braids against her chest. He set her sack of provisions on top, then opened the door for her.

"So," he said, "what's a young'n like you doin' so far from home?"

She stepped out into the late afternoon and looked eastward. The trail was busy with wagons coming and going and, so far, no horsemen appeared to be following her. She liked this trader — he seemed honest and hadn't cheated her — but she didn't want to tell him her business. What if Reverend McDuff or Mr. Carey showed up, asking him questions?

She took a deep breath and answered, "I prefer not to say. Thank you, kind sir, and good day to you."

CHAPTER SEVEN

———⟫◆⟪———

Indians

Only when Nessa returned from the trading post did she notice the Indian camp in the distance, beyond the river. There were clusters of tepees and the small shapes of children playing. On the far side of the riverbank, a brown-skinned boy sat on a pony and looked her way. She felt afraid. Would she and the sisters be attacked while they slept?

The driver saw her staring. "Don't worry about them," he said. "That's the Kaw tribe. Every time I see 'em, they been peaceful, thanks to a treaty. These ain't the ones to worry about. There're others busy stirring up trouble on the trail. To them, stealing horses is an honorable occupation."

Nessa considered this while spreading the hide in the grass to air out. She had heard people say the only good Indian was a dead Indian, but she didn't believe that was true. She recalled Miss Eva saying in class that all humans were created in the image of God.

A rustling of dresses interrupted Nessa's thoughts. The sisters were coming up the path from the river, using their parasols as walking sticks. Fanny Jo pointed to the buffalo blanket and asked, "What is *this?*"

Nessa suddenly realized it was the first thing she'd ever bought for herself and with her own money, too. She was elated with her purchase. But Fanny Jo begged her to return it to the trader.

"Please, dear," she said, "it's not civilized. Who knows where it's been or what sort of vermin live in it. And I must tell you it has a certain . . . odor." She glanced in the direction of Mr. Button and the driver to make sure they weren't watching, then she reached under the hoop of her wide skirt. After a moment, she removed a ten-dollar gold piece that she'd sewn into the hem before their journey.

"This will buy you several blankets," she said, offering it to Nessa.

But Nessa hid her hands in the folds of her dress. She didn't want to be rude to Fanny Jo, but she was not going to take her money and she would not go back to the trading post. She wanted to explain how the fur made her feel safe but couldn't find the words.

"I like the buffalo," Nessa finally told her. "It suits me."

Nessa lay on her side, wrapped in her buffalo robe, a cold breeze on her cheek. She was underneath the stagecoach with the sisters, who were snuggled together beneath the patchwork of their own quilts. The driver insisted they make their bed there for protection and that they turn in early for they would be leaving before sunrise the next morning. Nessa watched the low flames of the campfire where he and Mr. Button sat talking about President Lincoln's assassination. The rifle was between them. Nessa's stomach hurt with hunger, but it was a familiar feeling. For supper all she had eaten was a handful of apricots. She wanted her food to last as long as possible.

The rising moon was pale behind wisps of clouds and the air was filled with the aroma of wood smoke. Drumbeats came from the Indian camp, with singing. The voices were high and sharp and, to Nessa, they sounded angry. She burrowed into her robe. The fur felt soft against her face and reminded her of something from long ago. She closed her eyes and breathed in the scent that seemed so familiar. Had it been a dog she cuddled when she was younger? What was it?

She wished someone could tell her about her family.

At last, the robe's warmth made Nessa feel drowsy. Maybe, finally, she would be able to sleep. The drumbeats faded as a chorus of crickets rose from the brush and filled the night air with song. She wasn't as afraid as she had been a few hours ago. No one from the orphanage had followed her, and maybe the Indians across the river were peaceful after all.

Mr. Button and the driver had rolled themselves in their blankets without saying good night and were now snoring. Coals in the fire glowed red. The horses were picketed nearby and Nessa could hear them biting the grass and chewing. She wanted to pray, but she was so tired the words kept slipping away. "Dear Jesus," she began. Another moment passed as she struggled to stay awake. "Thank You for this warm bed. . . . Thank You that Mr. Carey is far, far away. . . ."

The Santa Fe Trail continued southwest across the open prairie. They traveled in the company of other wagons and traders who were well armed with rifles.

"Safety in numbers," their driver said.

Out the right side of the coach, Nessa saw scorched land in the distance, stretching to the horizon, as if there had been a fire. When she noticed the blackened areas moving, she thought perhaps they were shadows from clouds passing overhead. But the sky was perfectly blue and the sun was shining. There were no clouds.

"Buffalo," Mr. Button announced, looking up from a week-old newspaper about President Lincoln. "Thousands upon thousands. They are to the Indians what gold is to us."

Nessa tried to think of a polite way to ask why he knew so much, when Fanny Jo said, "May I inquire as to your occupation, Mr. Button?"

He snapped his newspaper, then creased it cleanly in half, then in quarters. "Certainly, ma'am," he said. "I'm a newspaper editor. My cousin and I are starting a weekly journal called *Prairie River News*, and we've got ourselves a ranch real near the fort. We came last spring to bring the printing press and other such, and to finish building our house. There're no telegraph wires yet, but we'll manage somehow, and what with all the traffic coming and going, we'll hear the news whether we like it or not. I've since made two additional trips, last summer and fall." Mr. Button unhooked his glasses from one ear, then the other, then folded them into his vest pocket.

"And may I inquire as to the nature of your business, ladies?"

The sisters took turns telling about their brothers, the war, and Fanny Jo's husband. Then Mr. Button looked at Nessa. His mustache lifted with his smile. "And how about you, young lady?" he asked.

In a fleeting second, Nessa thought of the story she wanted to tell: Her father was a brave soldier who saved a general's life during battle. Her mother was a poet but spent her days caring for her nine brothers and sisters. . . .

Suddenly, Laura cried out. Her face was pale as she pointed to the window. Mr. Button seemed alarmed. Holding his hat on with his hand, he leaned out to yell up to the driver. The wind blew his long mustache behind his ears.

"Indians!" he cried.

CHAPTER EIGHT

Fort Zarah

As the stagecoach sped up, there was an explosive rumble of wheels and thundering of hooves. The noise was deafening. Books and newspapers slid to the floor; satchels tipped over and spilled. Nessa fell into Mr. Button as she grabbed a hanging strap. They stared out the window in terror. Indians on horseback were racing along a nearby ridge.

Nessa's heart was in her throat.

The riders kept pace with the coach, but stayed their distance. Nessa could see that they rode without saddles and were barelegged except for moccasins. Many carried bows and wore a quiver bristling with feathered arrows over a shoulder. Others carried lances adorned with colorful beads and feathers; some had rifles.

They were close enough that Nessa could tell that two of the Indians were boys near her age, riding furiously fast, holding on with just their legs. Their braids, long and black, were bouncing off their shoulders. She was surprised that her fear was mixed with curiosity. She'd never seen such a spectacle.

Suddenly, the riders broke away and rode north, following a cloud of dust that had appeared beyond the ridge. In a moment they were gone, as if the prairie had swallowed them. The driver slowed the coach to rest the exhausted horses.

Mr. Button removed his hat to run his hand through his hair. "Buffalo hunters," he said, "at least that's all I think they were, thank God."

Fanny Jo slumped in her seat, holding her hand to her heart. Laura buried her face in her hands and began weeping. Nessa closed her eyes to gather herself. What if the Indians had been warriors or wanted to steal their horses? What had she gotten into by running away from civilization?

Later in the afternoon, soldiers on horseback appeared, wearing dark blue uniforms. They surrounded the coach and escorted it the last few miles to Fort Zarah. Nessa's spirits lifted to see the Stars and Stripes snapping in the wind. It was carried by one of the soldiers on a long pole that rested on his stirrup. Even this flag had black streamers.

Nessa and the sisters were shown to a laundress's tent where there were three cots. A mirror the size of a saucer was propped on a dresser. An officer's wife brought them a pitcher of water drawn from the well and invited them to freshen up. It had been a week since Nessa's birthday, the last time she had bathed. After splashing her face, she undid her braids and brushed out the snarls and dust, counting aloud one hundred strokes. Laura and Fanny Jo unpinned their hair, which fell in soft curls to their knees. They, too, brushed and counted, then twisted it up again with pins. Taking turns looking in the small mirror, they pinched their cheeks to bring color.

To their surprise, Mr. Button opened the flap and walked in. When he saw them grooming themselves, he flushed with embarrassment and swept his hat off his head.

"Please forgive me, ladies." He turned to leave.

"It's all right, Mr. Button," said Fanny Jo as she set down the hairbrush. "Were you going to tell us something?"

He rested his hat on his huge stomach. "Here's the schedule. Supper'll be served in an hour in the mess hall. Then at sunrise we leave for Prairie River — that is, Fort Larned. Depending on how our horses hold out, it'll probably take two days, meaning tomorrow night we'll camp near the river. I apologize if what I'm about to say worries you, but tragedy has struck that little town."

Nessa rose to her feet. Though she'd never been there, she already felt as if Prairie River was her home. "What happened?" she asked.

"Murder," he said. "The schoolteacher, a Mr. Smith, was shot. Not by Indians, thank God — what a political mess that would be — but by the Cooley Boys. The skirmish was out a-ways from the fort, so no one saw exactly what happened. Was he kin to you, young lady?" he asked Nessa.

She sat down on her cot again. "No, sir." She began braiding her hair. Two thoughts raced through her mind. One scared her, the other filled her with hope.

It upset her that outlaws were on the loose and would probably kill again. But on the other hand, it seemed as if Prairie River might be in need of a new schoolteacher. *Miss Eva tutored me well*, she thought. *Maybe this is something I'll be able to do.*

The next morning, Nessa was eager to be on the trail, for once again she had lain awake most of the night. It seemed the closer she came to her destination, the more unsettled she felt. *What if I've made a terrible mistake?* she kept asking herself. *What then?*

Soldiers from Fort Zarah escorted them as the stage followed the Arkansas River southwest. The prairie spread in every direction, as far as the eye could see. No mountains or trees broke the horizon, no Indian villages. The trail was dusty with teams of oxen and wagons headed for the Territory of New Mexico. Nessa held a handkerchief over her mouth to keep from coughing. She wished they were already there so she could take a bath and sleep in a soft bed.

At noon, they stopped to rest the team and eat from their dwindling provisions. When the soldiers finished watering their horses, the corporal saluted the stagecoach driver, climbed into his saddle, and led his men away, back to their fort.

"Guess we're on our own now," said Mr. Button.

Nessa kept her fears to herself. *Albert was right*, she thought. *We're in the middle of nowhere.*

The rest of the day passed without event. They stopped in early afternoon to make the journey easier on the horses. For supper, the driver roasted three black-tailed jackrabbits he'd shot and Nessa shared the last of her apricots. Their night under the stars was interrupted only by the sharp cries of coyotes and the lowing of cattle from travelers camped nearby. A gentle wind blew. Cooking fires glowed like lamps, reassuring Nessa that they were not alone.

CHAPTER NINE

Fanny Jo's Disappointment

The next day on the trail also passed without event.

The sun was low in the afternoon sky when Nessa saw an American flag in the distance. It seemed to stand alone on the empty prairie. When she pointed it out to Mr. Button, he sat up straight and said, "Yessiree, there she is, Fort Larned." He smoothed both sides of his mustache, ran his fingers through his hair, and put on his hat. "Home sweet home. Finally. Thank you, Jesus, amen."

Eight soldiers on horseback appeared from a ravine, loping onto a knoll and toward them, soon coming alongside the coach. Fanny Jo leaned out the window and shaded her eyes to see if any of the men in uniform was her husband.

"Not yet," she said, squeezing her sister's hand with excitement. "We're almost there, Laura. He's going to be so surprised to see us."

Mr. Button said, "Hooray for our boys in blue, that's what I say. They'll escort us right up to the door, so to speak. Don't know about you, but I'll be mighty glad to get out of this rolling chair."

As they neared the fort, Nessa saw that the flag was on a tall pole in the center of a field. Surrounding the field on four sides were tents and assorted buildings made of sod and wood. The trail came up to a smaller river, lush with cottonwoods and willows. The air felt cooler. A boy with a fishing pole waded in the shallows. He wore a soldier's cap that was several sizes too big, and playing in the water beside him was a large yellow dog.

"This here's Pawnee Creek," said Mr. Button as the coach rattled over a wooden bridge.

"Where's Prairie River?" asked Nessa.

"We just passed it." He pointed to a dried-up streambed that bordered one side of the fort.

"I meant the town," Nessa said. "Pardon me for interrupting, sir, but where is the town of Prairie River?"

"Well, it's right here," he answered. He swept his hand out the window, taking in the fort and a cluster of outlying sod buildings.

Nessa tried not to show her disappointment. She had pictured a real town with sidewalks and storefronts, a church with a steeple, and a schoolhouse. This was only a place for soldiers — a fort and a few shops. Her throat felt tight, but she swallowed hard to keep away the tears. Albert was right. Barely a dot on the map.

Fanny Jo had put on a yellow-laced hat and white gloves that reached to her elbow. She clutched the windowsill, looking out at the parade ground where soldiers were marching in formation. They could hear the roll of drums and a bugler. High above, the flag ruffled in the wind.

"Oh," she said. "Listen to the music — my word, I believe I see Edward!"

When the stage stopped, Mr. Button stepped out first so he could help Fanny Jo. "Allow me, ma'am," he said. It took a moment for her to gather her skirt and squeeze out the narrow doorway, followed by Laura. As Nessa grabbed the handle of her valise she felt sick to her stomach. She had no idea of what to do next.

A man in uniform greeted Fanny Jo, introducing himself as Sergeant Dann. He opened the notebook he was carrying and began searching for her husband's name. He ran his finger down one page then another, then looked up at her.

"Mrs. Holmes, I regret to inform you that your husband was transferred last week to the new fort being built west of here, Fort Dodge. It's nothing but dugouts along the river right now so there ain't a place yet for wives. And since he ain't assigned at Fort Larned no more, there's no quarters available for you here, neither. I'm sorry, but you'll have to —"

"What?" interrupted Fanny Jo. Her face was red and her voice quivered. "I'm sorry, what did you say? Fort Dodge? Where is that, sir?"

"Southwest of here, a two-day ride by wagon."

Fanny Jo put her gloved hand against the coach to steady herself. "But we've come all this way," she said. "It was going to be a surprise, wasn't it, Laura? Can't we at least go visit him? We could leave tomorrow."

The sergeant closed his notebook, sighed deeply, and looked at Mr. Button as if asking for his help. "Madam," said the soldier, "this prairie ain't New York City. There are five tribes of injuns around here; lots of 'em are *mad* at us white folks for various inequities. On account of this danger, the only way to get from here to Fort Dodge is by military escort, which leaves just twice a month, on the first and fifteenth. Until there's another stage headin' back east, you can find lodging in Suds Row — that would be those tents yonder for the washer ladies. They'll give you gals a cot till then. I'm sorry you came all this way for nothin', Mrs. Holmes. Good day." He touched the brim of his hat and walked toward a stone building with smoke curling out of its chimney.

Fanny Jo quickly took her sister's hand. "Mr. Button," she said, "we will be grateful if you could kindly show us to Suds Row. I am in need of some aspirin powder and a place to refresh myself."

"Yes, ma'am, I surely will."

Fanny Jo took a handkerchief from her sleeve to wipe her eyes. Seeing her tears, Nessa felt sorry she'd been irritated with the sisters. Their massive hoop skirts had taken up so much room inside the coach and they had kept the best seat for the entire journey, but these trifles didn't matter now. Nessa wanted to comfort Fanny Jo for she knew how it felt to be disappointed.

"Maybe things aren't as bad as they seem," she said. Nessa wanted to remind her that her sister was with her, and that at least she wasn't alone. But she kept the thought to herself. Meanwhile, Mr. Button bent down to search through his bag. This time when he offered his sock full of candy, Fanny Jo and Laura each took a piece.

CHAPTER TEN

A Little Town

It was dusk when the driver finished unloading the stage at the edge of Officers' Row. This was a line of tents and sod buildings with a wooden sidewalk in front. Candlelight shone in windows, and Nessa could hear piano music.

Two boys came out to help carry the sisters' trunks down to Suds Row. Mr. Button tipped them each a nickel, then paid them twenty-five cents to drag his trunk to a small office at one end of a warehouse. He then waved good-bye as he started the walk to his ranch, farther down Pawnee Creek.

Nessa watched Fanny Jo and Laura maneuver their wide skirts between tents as they introduced themselves to a lady and her daughter. The sisters hadn't invited Nessa to share lodging with them because, by not saying anything, Nessa had led them to believe her family was coming for her. Mr. Button believed this as well. They'd all said good-bye, agreeing to see one another in the morning.

The driver clicked his tongue to the horses and walked them to a corral. Nessa wanted to explore the fort —

which was shaped like a town square, with the large parade ground in its center — but realized she must find shelter for the night. Her bag was at her feet with her buffalo robe folded on top.

It was growing dark. She looked around her, wondering where she should go. Each side of the fort was as long as a city block. Since Mr. Button said this was a town, maybe there was a hotel or place to rent a room. With nine dollars left, she could at least pay for a few nights' lodging while figuring out what to do. As she walked toward one of the adobe buildings, she heard men's voices and through an open door saw bunk beds, but she turned around.

Barracks are no place for a girl, she thought. Looking across the field, she saw more buildings with soldiers out front. A blacksmith was working out of a canvas lean-to held up by poles.

It seemed the most friendly place would be Officers' Row. There were children playing out front, and Nessa breathed in the soothing aroma of supper cooking. When she stepped onto the sidewalk, she could see in one of the windows. A family was seated at a table, being served by a Negro woman. Nessa recognized the little boy as the one fishing down by the river, for he had the same soldier cap and the yellow dog lay at his feet. She took a deep breath, walked steadily to the door, and knocked before she could talk herself out of it. A Negro girl answered and then called to the missus.

The woman came to the door still holding her dinner napkin. "I'm sorry, but you can't stay here," she said. She was wearing a white linen dress, perfectly starched, and wore pearl earrings. Her hair was golden, swept up with ivory combs. "The laundresses will take you in. I'm sorry, dear." She smiled, but looked back toward her husband, who was calling to her with impatience.

As Nessa turned away, she suddenly felt feverish with exhaustion. Her throat burned as if she were coming down with a cold. The wind was stronger now, bringing clouds that darkened the twilight sky. She tried to remember when she had slept last. Council Grove, under the stagecoach? And before that? It felt as though she'd been awake for weeks.

Hunger gnawed at her and she was chilled by the churning air. From her valise, Nessa pulled out her shawl and wrapped it around herself, then found her last piece of hardtack, which she put in her mouth to savor. She picked up her things and headed toward the corral where there was a water trough and pump. Lifting the handle, then pulling it down, she tilted her head under the spout. Her face and braids got wet as the water splashed out, but she drank gratefully.

What should I do? She couldn't go to the laundresses' tent. Fanny Jo and Laura would learn the truth, that Nessa didn't have anyone to claim her. It was a humiliation she couldn't bear right now. She remembered Miss Eva's letter. Something about if you trust God, He will make your paths straight. But how does one *do* that? Nessa dried her face with her sleeve and started walking. When she felt the rain, she gazed up at the dark sky.

Dear Jesus, I'm so sorry if I've been foolish. . . . I thought I was doing the right thing, coming here, but now I don't know what to do. . . . Please show me where to go. . . . I'm scared. . . .

At the end of Officers' Row, she looked to the left. It was another block of adobe structures, now dark and quiet. Beyond the fort on the edge of the prairie was a stone building brimming with light. Nessa walked quickly in the rain to look through a window, but stood back so no one inside could see her. It was a trading post filled with barrels, crates, and shelves of canned goods. In the center was a billiard table where soldiers were playing. Two of them were poking each other with cues as if they were swords. Nessa didn't want to go inside. The rain was now pelting her, soaking her shoulders. She leaned into the wall for shelter, but the overhang was not even wide enough to protect a bird. In the other direction outside of the fort, there were more lights — another store, apparently. The door was open. She could smell cigar smoke and hear men cheering as if involved in some sort of a game. She didn't want to go there, either.

Nessa was shivering. Desperate to get out of the rain, she found herself hurrying along the bank of Pawnee Creek, toward another compound of lights. Soon, she saw a stone house. A lantern hung from a fence post, casting a welcoming light upon a protected porch where two men sat out of the wind, smoking pipes. Even from a distance, Nessa could see a sign that said, ROOMS TO LET.

Pressing against the wind, Nessa stopped twice to rest. The robe was heavy and her shawl kept slipping off her shoulders. Not wanting the men to see her, she hid in the shadows of a tree, listening. She was close enough to hear they were discussing the country's new president, a man named Andrew Johnson. They didn't appear to be outlaws and the house seemed safe.

She sat on her bag to think. *Do I go in here? What if I'm making a mistake?* When Nessa realized her feet were growing numb, she grabbed her things and headed for the porch. She was embarrassed by the noise her shoes made shuffling up the steps. The men paused their conversation to watch as she knocked on the door.

A wreath made from vines and black ribbons hung over a window. Another window was adorned with lace curtains. Nessa could see inside to a parlor where a man and a boy were playing checkers in front of the fireplace, which was framed by bookshelves. Quick footsteps came from the other side of the door, the latch rattled, and there stood a lady in an apron and gingham dress. She looked at Nessa with surprise, then grabbed her elbow to usher her inside.

"My word, honey," she began, "you shouldn't be outside with wet hair. A storm's coming, didn't nobody tell you? Come in by the fire, when was the last time you had something to eat? My name is Mrs. Lockett. . . ." She pushed open a door into the kitchen, brightly lit by a kerosene lamp hanging from a rafter.

A large iron stove was in a corner, its L-shaped pipe poking out of a wall, dishtowels and socks drying over its black stem. A tin tub for bathing hung against the wall above the coal bin.

The warmth was so inviting, Nessa didn't realize she'd

set down her things and was walking toward the stove with outstretched hands. Mrs. Lockett guided her to a chair nearby.

"Sit here while I get you some supper — oh, but your cheeks are burning up, dear, you must have a fever."

Her tender touch nearly brought Nessa to tears, but she quickly blinked them back. She was not about to cry in front of a stranger, and there was no reason to cry, anyway.

Mrs. Lockett set a tray in Nessa's lap. On it was a bowl of hot soup and a chunk of bread soft from melting butter. Nessa wanted to explain she fully intended to pay for this meal, but the next thing she knew, it was morning.

CHAPTER ELEVEN

———◆———

A View of the River

Nessa was in a bed in a tiny room. The ceiling slanted down to a window where sunlight made a square on the opposite wall. From downstairs came the sound of a heavy skillet being set on the stove, with an aroma of bacon and coffee. There were voices of men and women in conversation.

Nessa breathed deeply and recognized the scent of her buffalo robe. No wonder she was so comfortable. She lifted the robe to look at herself. She was in her nightgown! Her hands smelled fresh, like soap, and when she curled her knees to her chest she realized her whole body felt clean, even her feet.

How did I get here? she wondered. The dress she had worn on her journey was hanging from a peg on the wall. It looked freshly starched. The room was so small that she could lean over the bed and touch the other wall. There were two windows. When she looked out one of them, she was surprised to see nothing but green prairie. No buildings or houses. Nearby was the blue glimmer of Pawnee Creek that ran between high, twisting banks.

Cottonwoods and oaks shaded the bottomland. The other window looked out toward Fort Larned.

Nessa felt shy about going downstairs but knew she must. This would be the first time since she was four years old that she woke to a house full of strangers. What would she say? What if they asked questions she didn't know how to answer?

Quickly, she unpacked her valise, dressed, and made her bed — it was easy to just smooth the robe over the straw mattress — then folded her nightgown under her pillow with her Bible. A bureau by the door had a glass, a pitcher of water, and a bowl, which she used to wash her face. She poured herself a drink — and another — how thirsty she was! After putting on her apron and lacing her shoes, she stepped into the hallway, which had doors leading to other bedrooms. The voices grew louder as she came downstairs, then into the kitchen.

Mrs. Lockett saw her first and motioned for her to sit at an empty place at the long, oak table. She made introductions — there were two ladies and three men — then stopped, coffeepot in her hand.

"I didn't catch your name the other night, dear," she said.

"Nessa Clemens," answered Nessa, nodding to each person, trying to remember a name with a face. But she felt confused. "Did you say, 'the other night'?" she asked.

Mrs. Lockett set the coffee on the stove, then grabbed a stack of flapjacks from the warming oven. She put them on Nessa's plate, adding butter in between each steaming cake, then ladling hot syrup over the top. Nessa was so famished she didn't wait for Mrs. Lockett to answer, but with her fork dug into the pancakes for a huge bite. She closed her eyes at the buttery taste and thought, *This is the most wonderful, delicious thing I've ever eaten.*

"Yes," continued Mrs. Lockett, "what's it been now, Rolly? Two days?"

A boy Nessa's age had just come in from outside, carrying a bucket of coal. He smiled at her. "Two nights, Ma," he said. "It's the third day."

Nessa's fork stopped in midair. "Three?"

Rolly nodded. He had yellow hair that stuck out like hay and pale blue eyes. "You been sleepin' like a sissy," he said. "Got here Sunday, now it's Tuesday. And you missed the big storm."

"Never mind, son," said Mrs. Lockett, pouring a glass of milk for Nessa. Though she spoke loud enough for all to hear, the others politely ate their breakfasts, conversing among themselves. They were discussing the tragedy of Abraham Lincoln and wondering if his killer had been captured.

Nessa wanted to hear what they were saying, but turned to Mrs. Lockett. She had Rolly's same blue eyes, and her blond hair was swirled neatly atop her head.

"How did I . . . get into bed?" Nessa asked her, embarrassed at the thought of someone seeing her bare skin.

"Minnie, my daughter, helped. You can see her there coming up from the creek, fetchin' water." Mrs. Lockett pointed out the open back door. A six-year-old girl was walking up the path with a pail.

"Lordy," she said, "but you was faint with tiredness.

After you ate, we drew you up a warm bath by the stove, but you kept falling asleep. Finally, we dried you off — pardon my going through your bag, but it was me that put on your nightclothes — you could hardly stand, so we walked you upstairs to bed. Me and Minnie checked on you the next morning, but you slept on and on, bless your heart, and now here you are."

CHAPTER TWELVE

An Important Chore

When the guests got up from the table and left the kitchen, Nessa ate her last strip of bacon and finished her milk. How good it felt to have a full stomach. She knew it was dishwashing time and wanted to help, so she rolled up her sleeves and began stacking the plates and saucers. Minnie put the scrapings into a garbage pail to take outside for the hog.

Already Nessa had stayed two nights and two meals, yet hadn't paid a cent. She took four dimes from her shoe, where she had put them that morning while getting dressed. She did not want to be thought of as a beggar.

Mrs. Lockett poured scalding water from the stove into a dishpan of cool water. Nessa set her coins on the windowsill. "I don't know what you charge for board, but here's forty cents toward what I owe you." Nessa then started to scrub the plates with her knuckles.

"My dear, you are most kind," said the woman, "but guests don't do chores — that's what they pay me for. . . ."

"Mrs. Lockett — you see — I'm . . ." The word *des-*

perate came to mind, but she didn't want to say it. "Ma'am," she whispered, "if you would kindly let me earn my keep, I would be grateful. You won't be sorry."

Mrs. Lockett wiped her hands on her apron, then grabbed a towel from the stovepipe and began drying the dishes. She nodded toward a cupboard to show Nessa where to put them. Then without being told, Nessa gently hung the cups on hooks and carefully sorted the knives, spoons, and forks into a drawer.

"Well," said Mrs. Lockett, "I could use extra help in the kitchen, and there just might be something else you could help with — Rolly will show you. . . ."

Nessa sat next to Rolly in a small wagon, pulled by two mules. He drove alongside Pawnee Creek, which shimmered in the sunlight. Nessa liked the openness, how the prairie reached so very far and wide, and she liked the immense blue sky. The air was cool, but the sun on her shoulders made her feel warm. Yellow-breasted meadowlarks in song flitted up and away from the wagon's approach. From the grass came the clicking of insects. Nessa looked behind them and was startled that she could no longer see the fort, yet they had gone just a mile along this flat road.

Glancing at Rolly, she tried to think of something to say. A breeze fluffed out his hair like a dandelion and she could see a few blond whiskers on his chin. His knees poked through his trousers. It had always been easy for her to talk to Albert, for they'd known each other since they were young. But Nessa didn't know what to say to a boy she'd just met. She even felt too shy to ask where they were going and why.

Soon, Rolly turned away from the trail and drove into the tall grass that swished and brushed against the wheels. After a few minutes, they reached a clearing that spread in front of them for miles. Rolly pulled the reins and the mules stopped.

"Buff'lo," he said. "They were here a few days ago." He jumped down from his seat and grabbed some burlap sacks from the wagon. "Race you!" he said, tossing her one, then running ahead into the trampled grass.

Nessa hurried after him, still not understanding what was expected of her. When she saw him picking up clods of dirt, then tossing them into his sack, she bent down to do the same. But when she touched the ground, her fingers sunk into a pile of manure.

"Eew!" she said to herself. She had never heard of touching such a stinking mess and thought he was playing a trick. "Rolly?" she called.

"Buff'lo chips," he explained to her. "Look for dry ones; they burn better. And they're easier to pick up."

Nessa looked around at the treeless landscape and realized Rolly was gathering dung, not dirt. Prairie River wasn't like Missouri, with forests and woodlands and plenty of firewood. This must be how Mrs. Lockett wanted her to help, so she set to work. After an hour, they had filled ten sacks. Nessa's arms and back ached, and her hands smelled foul. And she was hungry again.

They pulled up to the barn when the sun was overhead, just as Mrs. Lockett stepped onto the back porch to ring the dinner bell. Nessa helped Rolly drag the bags into a shed, then washed her hands in the rain barrel that stood at the corner.

The guests were already eating when Nessa and Rolly seated themselves on the bench next to Minnie.

"It's up to the school committee. . . ." said a gentleman in a clean white shirt as he passed the butter.

". . . only six students . . ." said another.

". . . but the Cooley Boys . . ." said a woman. She helped herself to the potatoes, then offered them to the man next to her.

Nessa sat up straight. They were discussing the murdered teacher and the need for a new one. She listened carefully.

A meeting was to be held that afternoon at Applewood's. Three o'clock. It was one of the sutler stores that furnished supplies to the soldiers.

When the meal ended, Nessa grabbed her apron from a peg by the back door and started scraping dishes. She noticed Minnie under the table, wiping up gravy that had spilled through the cracks. Her eyes were blue and she wore her yellow hair in pigtails. Freckles covered her nose and cheeks. Nessa bent down with a rag to help her.

In a whisper Minnie asked, "Who hurt you?"

Nessa looked up from her rag. "What?"

"Me and Mama saw your scars." Still whispering, she said, "On the backs of your legs. We didn't look on purpose, but there they were, when you stepped out of your petticoat."

Then Nessa remembered the whipping. Mr. Carey had made her stand in the corner while the children watched. The humiliation had been unbearable. She had pressed her face against the wall until it was over. Miss Eva and Albert — good, sweet Albert — then carried her upstairs. Nessa's skirt was ruined, shredded from the whip. She hadn't forgotten about the scars, she just stopped thinking about them.

Before she could answer, Minnie changed the subject. "We ain't *never* supposed to wash up in the rain barrel like you did. That's clean water."

"Oh, I didn't know — I'm truly sorry."

"I won't tell on you," Minnie said. "Next time just use the dipper and pour into the pail there."

In her room, Nessa brushed her hair into fresh braids, then tied blue ribbons on the ends. She looked out the window that faced the fort and wondered where Applewood's was. The parade ground was busy with soldiers drilling. Rolly had explained that many of the people in Prairie River were civilians hired for different jobs to help at the fort. Nessa could see a boy carrying a box of groceries to Officers' Row and two little girls rolling a hoop with a stick. She also could see the trail where there seemed to be a constant arrival of freight wagons on the way to Santa Fe. She watched a stagecoach turn onto a smaller road along the creek as it approached the fort — the same as when she had arrived. This second entrance was designed so stagecoach passengers wouldn't have to step out into the dust and manure of so many oxen.

Suddenly, she felt overwhelmed. The committee meeting was in an hour and she had no idea of what to say. This was her first real day in Prairie River. More than ever, she wished Miss Eva were here, and Albert. For a moment she once again doubted having ventured so far into the wilderness alone.

Then she thought of Mr. Carey. Why had he insisted she marry Reverend McDuff?

Nessa closed her eyes. Despite her uncertainties, she felt a growing sense of peace that God had led her to Prairie River.

Dear Jesus, thank You for bringing me to Mrs. Lockett's boarding house. . . . Bless her for her kindness. . . . Now here I am, needing a way to take care of myself. . . . You know how I want to be a teacher like Miss Eva, and pay back her twenty dollars. . . . Please help me not feel so scared right now. . . . Also, could you please help Fanny Jo visit her husband, and bless Albert back in Missouri . . . ?

Nessa's prayer was long and heartfelt but ended when she caught herself daydreaming about a new dress and sunbonnet.

CHAPTER THIRTEEN

Dreadful News

A billowy white cloud drifted across the sun, making Nessa glad she'd worn her shawl. As she walked along Pawnee Creek toward the fort, she was better able to see the other buildings in the sutlers' compounds, now that it was daylight. Most were just one-story tall, built with layers of sod carved from the prairie. Nessa had never before seen grass growing out of the side of a house or from its roof.

The town was small enough that she walked the entire four sides in less than an hour, taking time to glance inside the open doorways and windows. In this time, she passed a baker's hut where one wall had racks stuffed with loaves of bread. In another, a Negro barber was shaving an officer. There were three blacksmiths working together, a carpenter's shop, then a storehouse where soldiers' uniforms, boots, and blankets were issued. She saw the barracks, a small library, a tinsmith, a tailor, and a stone building marked HOSPITAL. Sitting in the sunshine in front of a tent was a sail-maker, repairing a canvas top for one of the wagons.

By one of the stables, Nessa noticed the little boy in the soldier's cap. He was kneeling in the dirt, poking a stick into an anthill, his dog at his side. The boy saw the shadow of Nessa's dress and looked up at her.

"Excuse me," she said. "That's a mighty nice dog you have. Does it have a name?"

He put a protective arm around its neck. "I just call her Yellow Dog."

She smiled and bent down to pet the dog's head. "My name is Nessa, what's yours?" she asked the boy.

"Peter."

"Well, Peter, I was wondering if you could show me where the sutler's store is, Applewood's? I'm a bit lost."

By the time Peter had taken her to Applewood's, a wooden building on the outskirts of the fort, he had told her he was six years old, his sister, Poppy, was four, and his father, Lieutenant Sullivan, was friends with an Indian chief. He also shared numerous details about the insects he'd been observing. He gave Nessa a quick salute, then ran back to his project with the anthill.

Nessa's heart was in her throat when she opened the door. At the sound of a small bell jingling against the wood, several men stopped their conversations to stare at her.

"Nessa!" called a female voice. "Yoo-hoo, over here!" Three rows of chairs and benches formed a semicircle in front of the counter. Nessa was surprised to see Laura, and surprised she wore a simple calico dress with no hoops.

"Sit by me!" Laura said, patting the seat next to her.

Nessa was flushed with sudden happiness. It was the first time since her birthday — two weeks ago — that anyone had said her name. She wasn't alone after all.

"Oh, hello!" said Nessa. "Where's Fanny Jo? Are you staying in Prairie River for a while? I'm sorry, it's just that I'm so happy to see you. . . ." She touched Laura's dress, wanting to ask why she wasn't wearing her hoopskirt. But she did not want to appear nosy or overly curious about fashion.

Instead, Nessa asked, "What brings you to this meeting?"

Laura let out a long breath. "Well," she answered, "I'm seeking to be the new schoolteacher."

CHAPTER FOURTEEN

———⊰◆⊱———

The Long Meeting

Nessa wilted inside. She didn't have a chance against Laura, who was older and seemed smarter. So discouraged was she that if her seat hadn't been wedged between a tight row, she would have gotten up and left. A woman from dinner — Mrs. Bell — was sitting to her left. Her brown hair was braided on top of her head like a thick crown. She was pretty and quite large, completely filling her seat.

Nessa felt trapped. She wondered if she could pray to God right here, with her eyes open. Would He hear her?

The meeting started promptly at three o'clock, with Mr. Applewood standing behind the counter. Nessa watched him unfold his notes and put on a pair of spectacles, but in her mind she was talking to God:

Now what do I do? Why was I so bold to think I could be the schoolteacher? People will laugh if I say anything. . . .

The committee was a group of folks in town who had children. They wanted the school to continue despite the loss of their teacher. A discussion began about the Cooley Boys, which led to someone suggesting a bigger jail be built, which sparked a debate about the soldiers at Fort Larned.

"Gentlemen, please!" cried Mr. Applewood. "Some other time! We're here to interview Miss Laura Emmaline Sears."

The door opened with a jingling of its bell. The room grew quiet as everyone turned to see who had walked in. It was Mr. Button, red suspenders holding his trousers up over his stomach. His mustache curled alongside his plump cheeks. When he saw Nessa and Laura, he tipped his hat to them, then leaned against a shelf with his notepad and pencil.

Nessa was pleased to see Mr. Button for they'd spent many days together on the stagecoach. Then she remembered she had only made small talk with him and the sisters, not revealing anything about herself. They didn't know her, not really. Now she regretted having kept her distance. They wouldn't endorse her as a candidate for the position.

Mr. Applewood asked Laura to stand and face the crowd, so he could introduce her. He asked her to describe her qualifications, her age, why she wanted to teach, and so forth. Nessa could see Laura's hand at her side, nervously fingering her skirt.

"... earned my certificate last year in Pennsylvania. Am eighteen years old — let's see — I can read and write Latin. Parlor games, I love them — oh, yes — Fanny Jo and I are renting a room at the laundresses' until her husband, Lieutenant Holmes, is transferred back here." She told of graduating from an elite boarding school in Philadelphia and how her ancestors came to America on the *Mayflower*.

When Laura said her father had been a senator who sat on President Lincoln's cabinet, the crowd murmured with approval.

Nessa felt helpless. Not only was she jealous, she ached with longing. If only she knew who her parents were, maybe she, too, could impress people. If only she could get up and leave this horrible meeting without everyone staring at her.

Twenty minutes passed with more questions and answers. As Nessa listened, she compared herself to Laura. She felt small and unimportant. Then she recalled something Miss Eva told her: *Our lives are not an accident. God puts us where He can use us.*

Nessa considered these words. She realized it wasn't Laura's fault she was from high society. Now she felt sorry for thinking mean things toward her. She glanced up at Laura and noticed her hair had grown moist at the temples and a wisp from her bun had fallen across her eye. She'd been standing for nearly an hour and must be tired.

At last, Mr. Applewood folded his notes and tucked them into his pocket.

"Thank you, dear," he said to Laura. "You may be seated. Well, now, are there any objections? I reckon Miss Sears is suited to be our new teacher — everyone agree?"

A light applause rippled through the store. Nessa's heart began to race as she found herself slowly standing. Her chair scraped against the wood floor. On either side of her, Mrs. Bell and Laura shifted in their seats to look at her.

The crowd fell silent.

Mr. Applewood returned his eyeglasses to his nose to give Nessa a good look.

"Have we met?" he asked her.

"No, sir. My name is Vanessa Clemens." She cringed inside, remembering she didn't know her middle name.

"Is that your full name?" he inquired.

"Why, yes."

"What is it, then? Hurry up."

"I want to be your schoolteacher." Nessa was surprised by the strength in her voice.

The sutler lifted both hands in bewilderment, then turned to a man in the front row. They whispered for several moments. Finally, Mr. Applewood motioned for Nessa to come up front.

From where she stood by the counter, Nessa could not see everyone who had come to the meeting. In addition to those seated, a crowd had gathered in the doorway.

This store reminded her of the trading post at Council Grove, where she'd bought her buffalo robe. She liked the smell of spices and fresh-ground coffee and the colorfully labeled cans of pickles, beets, and corn. There seemed to be every type of food, tool, and household item anyone would ever need. Mr. Button still stood by the door, his pencil poised above his pad, ready to write what she might say. He gave her a nod of encouragement.

Never before had Nessa faced so many strangers.

Some of the women appeared to be officers' wives by the looks of their elegant hoopskirts. One man seemed impatient by the way he took out his pocket watch to check the time; others looked at her with curiosity. Mrs. Bell gave her such a friendly smile that Nessa took courage.

She avoided looking at Laura.

When Mr. Applewood asked about her qualifications she answered, "I like children and they like me."

He raised his eyebrows, shaking his head as if she'd given the wrong answer.

"And?"

"Well, I love to show children things I've learned and read stories to them."

"For crying out loud, little girl. What's your educational background?"

Nessa didn't want to explain about Miss Eva tutoring her at the orphanage or how she had been teaching Mary to read.

Mr. Applewood looked at the ceiling in exasperation. "Maybe you can tell us how old you are."

"Fourteen, just turned." At this, some men burst into laughter.

"You do realize," said Mr. Applewood, "that sixteen is when teachers get their certificates? What do your pa and ma think of this silly notion of yours? And where are they?" He stretched his neck as if to look high and low.

Nessa paused. She preferred to say nothing, but knew that sooner or later — if she wanted a real job and real friends — she must.

"They're dead."

Mr. Applewood sniffed. "So you're an *orphan*?" He said the word as if it were poison.

She nodded.

"And you came to Prairie River by yourself?"

"Yes, sir."

He spread his arms wide as if to take in the room. "Then who here, may I ask, knows a blessed thing about your character? Why, you don't even have a middle name — for all we care, you could be an accomplice of John Wilkes Booth. Even that murderer has a middle name."

Muffled laughter filled the room.

Nessa's jaw tightened. She felt the eyes of forty people on her and swallowed. She was not going to let them see her cry, especially this Mr. Applewood.

"I asked you, young lady, who here will speak on your behalf?"

Nessa watched Laura cross her ankles under her skirt. Mr. Button was writing in his notebook. Neither spoke.

Then a voice came from outside the store.

"I will."

CHAPTER FIFTEEN

New Friends

Mrs. Lockett marched through the store to the counter. Her arms swung at her side and her face was red with anger. Her swept-up hair bounced with her steps. People turned to watch her, whispering among themselves.

"Tom Applewood," she began, "you ought to be ashamed of yourself and this highfalutin meeting! Now, you listen to me — this girl, Nessa Clemens, is the first boarder under my roof that's shown backbone when it comes to hard work. And, meaning no disrespect to you, Miss Laura . . ." Here, Mrs. Lockett nodded toward Laura, who was sitting with her hands in her lap. Her face had gone pale.

". . . meaning no disrespect," she continued, "but just because Nessa here ain't got folks to help her ain't no reason to think she's shifty. I reckon Nessa would make Prairie River proud as our schoolteacher so I am standing here to tell you so."

Mr. Applewood backed up several steps. "Good Lord, Vivian," he said, "you surely do give a man a fright. Of course, we trust your judgment with these travelers. Always have. We'll think upon what you have said in the coming hours. Meeting adjourned!"

The store erupted with voices and the thumps of men moving chairs and benches. Nessa watched Mr. Button hurry across the way to his newspaper office. She looked for Laura, but saw only her profile outside as she passed by the window. She wanted to speak with her and apologize if she'd upset her.

Nessa stood by the counter with Mrs. Lockett, who was purchasing flour and a crate of canned peaches. She and Mr. Applewood conversed as nicely as if there'd never been a harsh word between them.

"Thank you, Tom," she said. "Add this to my account, please." She smiled at Nessa, who held the sack of flour.

Rolly was there to carry the crate back to the boarding-house. He grinned at Nessa. "You ain't no sissy anymore," he said.

Nessa wrapped two towels around her hands, opened the oven, and took out a heavy, rectangular pan of peach cobbler. With a knife, she gently poked the golden crust, as Mrs. Lockett had shown her, then when the knife slid out clean she knew it was baked through and through. Its aroma of sugary cinnamon and vanilla made the back of Nessa's mouth water.

"Leave it by the window to cool and come eat your supper," Mrs. Locket called to her. She set Nessa's plate down between Minnie and Rolly and continued to circle the long table with heaped platters of fried pork, turnips, biscuits, and gravy.

Three men had arrived on the afternoon stage from Fort Zarah. They sat on the bench with Mrs. Bell, who took up enough room for two people. Nessa liked Mrs. Bell. Her brown eyes were gentle like Albert's, and her smile made Nessa want to be her friend.

"We have ourselves a brave girl," Mrs. Bell announced, patting Nessa's hand. Then she explained to the new-comers the events of the day. In a pleasant, cheerful man-ner she engaged the men in conversation about the importance of education. By the time Nessa got up to help with dessert plates, Mrs. Bell had also told the his-tory of Prairie River and had even described the sod house her husband was building nearby.

"He's one of the blacksmiths in town, you know," she said. "Our home should be ready in time for the baby." Nessa felt herself blush. Now she understood the term "to be heavy with child." This topic of where babies come from was something she once asked Miss Eva. But they were both so shy, they had dissolved into nervous giggles and changed the subject. Because Mrs. Bell was expect-ing, Nessa was now more curious than ever.

Nessa surveyed the kitchen. It was warm from the stove and from eight people talking, eating, and laughing. Though most of them were strangers to one another, there was a friendliness that made Nessa feel welcome.

When she noticed steam escaping from under the coffeepot lid, she got up to move it to the back of the stove so it wouldn't boil over, then took cups from their hooks to pass around, with saucers. From the cupboard, she took out the sugar bowl. It was blue-and-white china with a domed lid and it matched the pitcher of cream. She set both in the center of the table. With a steady hand she poured coffee into each cup, careful not to drip.

Her gratitude toward Mrs. Lockett was deep and the only way she knew how to express it was to help as much as possible. Nessa didn't want to disappoint her.

It was on her mind, though, every moment, to be cautious. To not make any mistakes. Mr. Carey had not tolerated mistakes.

Once Nessa had been carrying a tray to him in the parlor where he read his newspaper. Her apron pocket had accidentally caught on the doorknob as she passed the entry. Before she could catch herself she had fallen forward, landing hard on her knees. Pain had prevented her from getting up right away. As she lay on the floor, she was eye level with the teacup as it struck the brick hearth and shattered. Cookies had tumbled onto the soaked rug.

"You . . . you little . . ."

Nessa had closed her eyes, expecting a blow, but none had come. From the floor she watched his shiny black boots stomp from the room into the hallway. Albert was there immediately to help clean up the mess. She had wept, not from pain but from frustration. It seemed she always did something wrong.

"Hey, look at Noah's flood," called Rolly, interrupting

Nessa's thoughts. He pointed to the table. Nessa was horrified to see she had emptied the coffee into the bowl of mashed potatoes.

"Oh, no," she cried. "I'll clean it up — I'm so sorry. . . ." But before she could grab a towel, Rolly lifted the overflowing bowl and tipped it into the bucket Minnie had brought over to him. She then carried it out the back door for the pig's trough.

"I'm sorry," Nessa said again. She wanted to cry with embarrassment. How could this have happened when she was trying so hard to be careful? The guests and Mrs. Bell were applying their own napkins to the wet table, still talking cheerfully among themselves.

"It's all right, dear," Mrs. Lockett told her, taking the coffeepot from her hand. "Last Sunday, Rolly knocked over a pan of chocolate pudding right onto the visiting minister and his wife. It was a bigger to-do than this one.

"But listen here, honey, messes we *can* clean up. I don't cry over those no more."

CHAPTER SIXTEEN

Front-page Story

Next morning after putting away the breakfast dishes, Nessa helped Rolly on the south side of the barn. His yellow hair was askew and he wore the same trousers with holes at the knees. Though his arms were thin, he was strong, easily lifting and emptying the sacks of buffalo chips. He gave her a rake and together they spread the manure in the sun, under an overhang protected from rain.

"This stuff stinks when it burns," he told her, "but come winter we'll be glad for it. There's wood from the river, but the army uses most of it. Do you mind goin' with me tomorrow, Nessa, to get more chips? We gotta keep gathering till it snows. Oh, I almost forgot — lookee here — Mr. Button gave me this when I was in town." He pulled a square of brown paper from his pocket and unfolded it.

It was a newspaper. The headline, in big block letters, said:

ORPHAN NEW TO PRAIRIE RIVER
IN TIE FOR SCHOOLTEACHER

WITH SENATOR'S DAUGHTER
FINAL VOTE SEVEN O'CLOCK THIS EVENING
PIE SOCIAL FOLLOWING
COME ALL

The article was brief, describing Miss Laura Sears as "refined" and "from back East." Nessa was said to be "plucky." It was the first time she'd seen her name in print. She didn't know if it was good or bad to be plucky, but she liked the sound of the word. She read the story aloud to Rolly.

He smiled. "During the war we didn't get much schoolin', for one reason or another, so I hope you get to be our teacher," he said. "That Miss Laura talked a lot of fancy words, but didn't say nothin' about learning."

Nessa folded the newspaper into her sleeve. "I hope so, too, Rolly."

That afternoon, Nessa walked to Suds Row where there was a cluster of sod buildings and tents by the river. A cauldron of water was steaming over a campfire. Two clotheslines strung between posts were laden with an assortment of blue trousers and shirts flapping in the wind.

Through a gap between buildings she could see across the fort's parade ground to the prairie beyond, still green with new growth. The sky was turquoise. Nessa knew the smudge on the horizon was buffalo grazing and that she and Rolly would drive the wagon there tomorrow on their errand.

A sound of female voices drew her attention away

from the view. Nessa pressed her ear to the door of one of the huts, but because someone was crying she couldn't hear all that was said.

". . . don't know *what* we'll do . . ."

". . . it was your idea. . . ."

". . . don't blame me . . ."

". . . wish we'd never . . ."

". . . if Father finds out, who knows what he'll . . ."

Nessa's eyes grew big. She was sure this was where the sisters were staying. What were they talking about? Should she come back later? She waited a moment, then knocked. The voices stopped. Nessa could hear rustling and footsteps.

"Who's there?"

"Hello — it's Nessa."

The latch clicked. Fanny Jo peeked out, then opened the door to let her in. Sunlight from a south window made the room seem cheerful except that it was quite small — just large enough for two cots, a chair, and a tiny wood-burning stove. And it was a mess. Clothes were strewn across the beds. Petticoats and corsets were piled in a corner. The dirt floor was littered with shoes, stockings, scarves, and gloves. The sisters' long hair hung to their knees in tangles and their eyes were red. Nessa was surprised by how young the sisters looked without cosmetics and realized Fanny Jo was barely older than Laura.

"I came to say — that is — I hope you . . ." Nessa wanted to talk about yesterday's meeting, but was distracted by the scene before her. It was obvious they had been fighting. "Please excuse my asking," she said, "but is everything all right?"

The sisters glared at each other, then Fanny Jo started weeping.

Nessa sat by the window as they told their story.

A week after arriving in Prairie River, Mr. Button arranged to drive a wagon for the sisters, with some camping supplies for the two-day journey to Fort Dodge. Six soldiers from the Kansas Cavalry escorted them.

Fanny Jo's eyes again filled with tears. She sank into a chair, her face in her hands. Not knowing what to do, Nessa knelt beside her and picked up a hairbrush from the floor. She began brushing her long hair, gently untangling the snarls.

"Your husband . . . is he . . . ?" Nessa was going to say "dead?" but didn't want to speak the word.

"He doesn't want her," Laura answered. "He sent her away. He told us to go back to Pennsylvania."

Nessa stayed in the sisters' room as the afternoon sunlight shifted across the floor. She picked up things from the floor, arranged shoes on a low shelf, hung petticoats on hooks, folded dresses and shawls into their trunks. On the table there was a loaf of bread and wedge of cheese. Nessa made up a platter of food with dried apple slices and poured them each a glass of water from the pitcher. The stove had warm coals. She wanted to boil water for tea, but there wasn't enough kindling to stir into flames.

All the while she busied herself, Fanny Jo sat in her chair, weeping. Laura lay on the bed, staring up at the ceiling.

"We can't possibly return home," Laura said to no one in particular.

Several minutes passed. "I have to go now," Nessa finally said. "It's time for me to help Mrs. Lockett." She wanted to ask more questions, but didn't want to pry.

As she closed the door behind her and walked down the stairs, she knew in her heart there was something the sisters hadn't told her. Perhaps this was one of those messes that is not easily cleaned up.

CHAPTER SEVENTEEN

The Vote

After supper, Mrs. Bell and Mrs. Lockett went to Applewood's Store. The school committee would be voting for the new teacher, but Nessa stayed home. She did not want to hear people discussing her, good or bad. She did not want someone to remind her that she didn't know her middle name.

Meanwhile, as the evening wore on, the guests relaxed in the parlor. Rolly played chess with one of the gentlemen and Minnie drew in her diary. Nessa sat at Mrs. Lockett's rolltop desk, in an oak swivel chair with arms. Among the cubbies there were envelopes and sheets of tissue-thin paper, a jar of black ink, and sharpened quills that were there for everyone's use.

A stage was leaving in the morning, headed east, and would be taking mail.

Nessa wrote a new letter to Albert and folded it inside one to Miss Eva, enclosing one paper dollar toward the twenty she owed her. She trusted Miss Eva to deliver Albert's letter without peeking. To seal the flap, she dripped candle wax over it. This way she could send both letters for a dollar, which was the postage from here to Independence.

At first, she considered not telling her exact whereabouts, but she wanted Miss Eva and Albert to know. She was certain they would not tell Mr. Carey or Reverend McDuff. Prairie River was small enough that people could find her, anyway, just by coming to town and asking. So Nessa wrote about her new home with Mrs. Lockett and asked Miss Eva to please tell the children she missed them.

She'd been so busy and so tired from the journey that only now did she think about her young friends in the orphanage, picturing each one of their faces, Mary especially. She closed her eyes for a moment, praying for God to protect them. Then she shocked herself by praying that Mr. Carey would die. Her eyes flew open.

I'm sorry, Jesus. . . . Help me forgive him. . . . I don't hate him . . . not really . . . not much . . .

In her letter to Albert, Nessa said Kansas was the most beautiful place she'd ever seen.

She described the town, how it was really an extension of Fort Larned. And how it sat in an elbow of Pawnee Creek, protected from attack on those two sides. On a third side was a huge gulch called an oxbow because of its winding shape. Nessa liked the fact that folks here were optimists. First, because they called this oxbow Prairie River, when it was really just a dried-up streambed. And second, because they called their tiny outpost a town, when most of its habitants were soldiers and horses.

There were no mountains, she reported, but there was a swell to the land that rippled with tall grass touched by wind.

"The sky is the color of Mary's eyes," she wrote. "It reaches higher than I can see, and it goes forever, as far as the East is from the West. I wish you could see it, Albert. Now my favorite colors are blue and green. Blue for the sky and creeks, green for new grass."

Nessa dipped her quill in the bottle, then tapped it against the inside to catch the drips. She looked over her shoulder to where Minnie sat with her journal in her lap. She was drawing a sunflower. Nessa wanted to ask if she and Rolly had a father, but didn't want to take the chance of upsetting her. She decided to wait.

After going to the outhouse, she went upstairs to her room, undressed, brushed her teeth with water, then blew out her candle. In the darkness, she looked out her window. The prairie was black. Brilliant starlight touched the horizon, as if God had pulled down a speck-led shade. A serenade of frogs rose in the cool air. Nessa loved their rhythmic calling to one another.

In the other direction, she could see someone carrying a lantern along Officers' Row. At Applewood's, the door was open, spilling light outside onto the dirt. Soon people would be voting.

Nessa left her window open for fresh air, then crawled into bed. Her buffalo robe was warm and made her feel as if she were home, though she had no memory of her true home. She thought about the sisters and wondered what their real story was. She would tell no one about their predicament, but now she understood that Laura was probably as desperate for the schoolteacher position as she was.

And what about Fanny Jo's husband? How could a man be so cruel as to send his wife away after she'd traveled so far?

But Nessa remembered Miss Eva telling her there were always two sides to a story. She had a feeling the sisters hadn't explained everything.

Nessa woke before dawn to the aroma of freshly baked bread. In the dark, she tidied her room while glancing outside. She could hear a bugler playing reveille. By now she knew this song meant "time to get up," and in minutes the soldiers would be lined up in front of their barracks for roll call.

When she went downstairs, Mrs. Lockett was already at the stove, pulling out a large loaf of rye bread.

"Morning, Nessa," she said. "If you'd like, you could gather a couple dozen eggs for me — but you probably want to hear the news first. . . ."

"Yes, ma'am."

"Well, the meetin' went on till eleven with that scoundrel, my friend Tom Applewood, stirring things up about orphans just being trouble and so on — don't you worry, honey, me and Mrs. Bell set him straight — but I am sorry to tell you the vote went for Miss Laura Sears."

Nessa tied on her apron, shrugging. "It's all right," she said. "Laura needs the work more than I do. I mean, she's older than I am, she studied to be a teacher. . . ." Nessa stopped herself before revealing any more. She took the egg basket from a shelf and rushed outside.

The cold air surprised her, as did the immensity of dark sky still pricked with stars. "Oh," she whispered, "it's so beautiful." She wished Albert could stand here with her on this fresh morning of a new day.

Attached to the barn was the henhouse, a sod hut big enough for her to stoop inside and walk hunched over to gather eggs. It was warm and smelled like moist feathers.

While she gathered the still-warm eggs, Nessa thought about her life so far in Prairie River. She wasn't as disappointed as she thought she'd be when she'd first arrived there.

First, a family had invited her to stay with them. They were giving her food and a cozy bed simply in exchange for her helping with chores. Second, her secrets seemed small compared to Laura's and Fanny Jo's. And last but not least, she still had about three dollars.

After raking out the barn, Nessa took her enthusiasm to town. She wanted to congratulate Laura and show her there were no hard feelings.

This morning, she'd brushed her hair into one thick braid down her back, with a white bow on the end. She liked how it matched the buttons and collar of her dress.

As she came to the sutler's store, she saw a woman out front sweeping the wooden steps.

"Good day, Mrs. Applewood," she said while opening the door to go inside.

The woman leaned on her broom to look at her. Her face was thin and frowny, as if she had just smelled sour milk. Her hair was pulled back into a tight bun.

"Well, well, well," she said, "if it ain't the little orphan. What's your business here?"

Nessa felt her cheerfulness ebb. "Oh, I just want to look around," she said.

"That so?"

"Yes, ma'am."

"Well," the woman said, "folks around here don't take kindly to strangers with mysterious lineage. Keep your hands off our merchandise or I'll wup you myself, don't think I won't."

Nessa felt as if her heart were boiling. She wanted to say something nasty, to make the woman just as upset as she was. Her thoughts raced with ugly words.

"Mrs. Appleworm," she began, but nothing came to mind that could set things right. Suddenly, a horrible realization floated over her. Instead of "Applewood," Nessa had mistakenly said "Appleworm," and she had put the emphasis on *worm*.

It just slipped out and hung in the air between them, the shock on the woman's face the only evidence.

"Uh-oh," said Nessa, taking her hand off the door's latch, "I . . . didn't mean to say that — ma'am, I'm sorry. . . ." She hurried away, furious at herself. If only she'd kept her mouth shut, she wouldn't have needed to apologize to that unpleasant woman.

CHAPTER EIGHTEEN

Teacher's Problem

The schoolhouse sat in a clearing near a creek, one mile from town. It was actually a storage building on Mr. Button's ranch. He and his cousin had cleaned it out for the community to use since Fort Larned didn't yet have one of its own. Also, on Sundays it served as a church.

Six weeks were left of the spring term, two weeks having been lost between Mr. Smith's murder and the hiring of Laura. His salary had been twelve dollars a month; hers would be ten.

"Here's your lunch, honey," Mrs. Lockett said, handing Nessa a small pail with a lid and wire handle. Inside was a meat sandwich, hard-boiled egg, brownie, and dried fig. "I'm gonna miss having you around all day, but I am mighty pleased you'll be in school."

After scrubbing the breakfast pans and drying them, Nessa hung up her apron, grabbed her pail, and walked with Minnie and Rolly. For part of the way, they followed the road they'd taken when hunting for buffalo chips. The countryside was alive with songbirds and the high, inquisitive trill of prairie dogs. Tiny white butterflies flitted in the brush. Soon, the road veered off, onto a path so narrow they had to walk single file through dew-drenched grass that grew up to their knees. By the time they reached the school, Nessa's hem and stockings were soaked.

This was unlike her classroom at the orphanage, which had been gloomy. Here, the walls were thick layers of sod, whitewashed inside. Morning sunlight streamed in the east windows and out through the open door, which faced west. A small black stove was in a corner of the room, but was not heated this morning. There were twelve desks, four rows with three in each row, with benches along the walls. The teacher's desk was in front of the blackboard. In another corner was a stool, Nessa guessed, for misbehaving students; another corner held a crate filled high with buffalo chips.

A small boy burst into the room. Nessa was happy to see her new friend Peter. He was late, but he stopped by the door to hang up his soldier's hat. When he noticed Nessa, he came to her desk and motioned her near, as if he wanted to say something to her. She leaned over so he could cup his hands by her ear.

"Yellow Dog is gonna have puppies," he whispered. Then he ran to his seat in the front row, next to Minnie. He turned around once more to smile at Nessa.

Laura stood in front of the class, waiting for everyone to be still. She seemed nervous, for she looked here and there and kept clearing her throat. Nessa could tell she was wearing a corset under her dress because her waist was pinched like an hourglass. Her front buttons went up to her chin and her hair was brushed up neatly with combs, like Miss Eva's.

"Good morning, boys and girls," she said. "I'm your new teacher. You may call me Miss Laura."

No one responded to the greeting except Nessa, who answered, "Good morning, Miss Laura."

Three children Nessa hadn't seen before introduced themselves to Miss Laura: a large twelve-year-old boy named Howard, then two girls, Augusta and Lucy. Nessa sat in the back row with Rolly because at fourteen they were the oldest.

After the introductions, Howard leaned over his desk to spit on the floor. "That's what I think about *that*," he said.

Laura was startled. "Whatever do you mean?"

"School. It's for the birds."

Laura's brown eyes grew wide. "Well," she said after a moment, "I suppose you may be excused then, Howard. Anyone else unhappy being here today?"

Lucy raised her hand.

"Yes?"

"My shoes are wet, I have a blister — and I need to use the privy."

"I see. Anyone else?"

Augusta raised her hand, then stood up when Miss Laura called on her. "My ma's gonna have a baby any minute and I want to be there to help."

"How old are you, Augusta?" asked Miss Laura.

"Eight."

"And you, Lucy?"

"Seven."

"Very well, then, you both may be excused. Just make sure to close the privy door when you're done. Augusta, go help your mother. Lucy, you run all the way home so your feet warm up and never mind about the blister. It will soon pop, then turn to a callus, never to bother you again."

Nessa was astonished to see the little girls get up, take their lunch pails, and head outside, Miss Laura cheerfully waving them off. Howard was still in his seat, shuffling his feet over a stick that he purposefully had dropped on the floor. It made an annoying *click-click-click* sound, again and again. Nessa wanted to kick him so he would stop but did not want to risk getting in trouble her first day. She waited for Miss Laura to do something.

Finally, Miss Laura said, "Howard dear, what's troubling you? I said you may return home. Would you rather go outside and play with Peter? Peter, how would you like to have a nice long recess and play any game you like with the other boys?"

Peter jumped up. "I'd like that plenty, Teacher. Can I go now?"

"Indeed you may. Perhaps you can see who runs the fastest, or who can jump over the narrow part of the creek. Then come tell me who won."

Peter dashed out the door with a grin on his face. Nessa glanced at Rolly, who was slowly raising his hand.

"Yes, boy, what is it? Say your name again."

"It's Rolly Lockett, Miss. . . . Pardon me, but I don't want to play at the creek. I can do that at home. Ain't you gonna teach us something?"

Miss Laura waved good-bye to Howard as he left to join the smaller boy. She no longer seemed nervous, but she ignored Rolly's question.

Now Minnie raised her hand. The back of her head had a neat part down the middle to divide her pigtails. Nessa thought the red ribbons on the ends were pretty in her blond hair.

"Yes?"

"My tooth is loose," said Minnie. "See? And I gotta use the privy, too."

"Then you may be excused."

It was Minnie's turn to jump up and happily head down the aisle for the door. When she came to Rolly's desk, he stuck out his arm to stop her.

"I ain't letting you walk home by yourself," he told her. "You're only six."

"Well, I ain't staying if Teacher says we don't have to." She struggled out of his grasp and ran to pick up her dinner pail.

Rolly threw his palms up in frustration. "Mother will not be happy about this, not one bit. Nessa, I don't want you walking home alone, neither. . . . Will you come with us, then?"

Nessa looked at Miss Laura, who still stood at the front of the classroom, her hands now folded at her thin waist, a dreamy look on her face. She was pretty in her fine dress and lace collar. Her high-buttoned shoes were of soft leather. It seemed that Laura should be in one of those paintings of a lady gazing out a tall window.

"I guess I'll leave now, too," Nessa said to her.

As she took the path with Rolly and Minnie, she looked behind her at the little schoolhouse alone on the prairie. Miss Laura was standing in the doorway, gazing up at the towering white clouds.

CHAPTER NINETEEN

—=>•⟨=—

Another Chance

his won't do a-tall," Mrs. Lockett said when Rolly told her about their school day.

They were eating noon dinner with Mrs. Bell and five new guests who were much interested in this dilemma.

"Why do you think the teacher dismissed her students?" one of the men asked.

Minnie shrugged so big her shoulders came up to her ears. "I dunno. She's plenty nice, though."

Rolly poured gravy over his mashed turnips, then passed it to Mrs. Bell. "Maybe she don't know how to teach," he said. "Why, I didn't see one book on her desk, not even a dictionary or Bible like Mr. Smith had."

When the bread came to Nessa, she took a piece and spread it with soft butter. "I think Miss Laura's afraid," she said. "Big Howard's only twelve, but she's scared of him. Plus, she wants everyone to like her, so it was just easier for her to let us go home."

"See what I mean?" said Rolly. He pointed his spoon

at Nessa. "Didn't I tell you she didn't say nothin' about learning at that meeting? Didn't I say *you* should be our teacher, Nessa?"

The room fell quiet. Nessa was certain she blushed, for her cheeks felt hot and she was at a loss for words. Now it was her turn to shrug.

"Miss Laura needs this position," she said.

"Oh?" asked a gentleman guest. "Why is that?"

Nessa stared down at her plate. Suddenly, the beef and baked beans — her favorite — didn't seem appetizing. Why did the sisters have to have a big secret? Why must she be the one to know some of it?

Mrs. Bell asked gently, "Nessa, dear, is anything the matter?"

In a voice just above a whisper she replied, "Meaning no disrespect to any of you, I prefer not to say."

An emergency school committee meeting was held that evening after supper. Once again Nessa stayed away and occupied herself in the parlor. Minnie sat on the rug in front of the fire, dressing her doll. She had finally wiggled her front tooth enough so that it fell out on their way home. She was proud of herself and kept sticking her tongue out through the hole.

It was getting easier for Nessa to talk with Rolly now that she realized how eager he was to learn. The shelves on either side of the fireplace were full of leather-bound books, magazines, and dime novels.

When she saw how often he pulled something out after chores and sat down to read by candlelight, she thought, *He is a true student.*

"What's your favorite subject, Rolly?" Nessa asked.

"Oh, near everything — I like poems by Walt Whitman, stories about ancient Rome. I like to watch stars at night and wish I could sail on a ship at sea. I like the Bible, but only read parts of it so far — my pa would read it to us at night before he left. . . ."

Rolly got up to push the game table over to Nessa between their chairs. From a narrow wooden box, he emptied the checkers and began arranging them onto the board.

"Best out of five wins, all right?" he asked her.

But Nessa wanted to know more about his father. As they made their first moves, Nessa studied his face to see if he was upset or eager to talk. He had the same freckles over his nose and cheeks as Minnie, and his hair hadn't seen a brush in days. His knees were a bit farther out the holes in his trousers than before. If Nessa could have any brother of her choosing, she would pick Rolly.

"Your father," she began, "where did he go?"

"To the war," came the answer as he quickly slid a checker forward.

Nessa swallowed, afraid to ask the question.

Rolly took his eyes off the board to look at her. "We ain't heard from him since his letter from Gettysburg. Ma is scared he was kilt, but Mrs. Bell thinks he could be in a hospital. We read the papers, but so far ain't seen his name. It's been such a long time since we seen him last — triple jump — gotcha, Nessa!"

Three days passed without school. Parents on the committee didn't know what to do. On the third evening, after supper and a pie social, they held another vote.

The clock on the mantel was chiming nine times as the front door opened. Most of the guests had gone upstairs to bed, but Nessa and Rolly were still in the parlor talking. Minnie had fallen asleep on the rug, covered by a knit blanket.

Mrs. Lockett came in with Mrs. Bell to warm themselves by the fire. They stood with their backs to the coals, both smiling at Nessa.

"Well, my dear," said Mrs. Bell. "You'll never guess who is on his way over here to ask you a question."

Nessa gave them a quizzical look, then turned toward the front door where someone was knocking.

"Come in!" called Mrs. Lockett.

In walked Mr. Applewood. He was not smiling. When he saw Nessa, he came near her chair but looked at her shoes instead of her face.

"Vanessa Clemens," he began, "the school committee has finally made a decision. We've spoken to Miss Laura Sears and she's agreed you may be more suited for the position. She confessed that her only experience was tutoring at a private academy and she isn't prepared to teach in a one-room schoolhouse. Though you are young and a stranger to most of us, Prairie River needs a teacher right away, and we're asking you — that is, if you're still interested — the salary will be nine dollars a month. . . ."

Mr. Applewood took a breath to continue his speech.

"Mind you, this is just until the end of the term, until we can find someone better. We figure you need something to do with your time — as they say, idle hands are tools for the devil's workshop."

He looked up, but only as far as her shoulder. "Could you let us know your decision by tomorrow morning?" At that, Mr. Applewood left the room, closing the front door quietly behind him.

Nessa felt her mouth drop open. She didn't know how to respond. It felt as if she'd just been insulted, but then he also had offered her a job.

Mrs. Lockett headed for the kitchen and grabbed her apron from the peg. "There's fresh pecan pie warming on the stove," she called. "We ain't goin' to bed without celebrating."

The kitchen was warm. Nessa sat at the table with Rolly and Minnie. Mrs. Bell poured fresh cream into a bowl and whipped it with a fork until it was filled with air. Then she spooned it onto the slices of pie Mrs. Lockett was setting on the table. A gentleman guest who had been dozing in a parlor chair, his book upside down on his lap, woke up and now joined them. His wife came downstairs in her wrapper after hearing the commotion.

"Oh, isn't it wonderful that Nessa's to be our school-teacher?" said Mrs. Lockett. "You are going to say yes, aren't you, honey?" She set the coffeepot in the center of the table with cups and saucers so those who wanted some could help themselves.

Nessa picked the pecans off the top of her pie and ate them one by one. With her spoon she scooped up the whipped cream to savor. She felt a mixture of excitement and something she couldn't quite understand.

This is what she had prayed for — to be Prairie River's teacher. But when the position had been given to Laura instead, even though she was disappointed, Nessa had tried to make the best of things. Now, after a puzzling three days, it was being given to her after all. Is this what God intended all along?

And, if this was such good news, why did she feel a sense of dread? The happy chatter of the guests filled the room while Nessa considered this. She ate a second helping of pie and drank a cup of coffee.

The answer came to her.

It was because she'd gotten a glimpse of her students. Big Howard was taller than she was and eager to make trouble. He could easily thrash her if he wanted. Then there were the others. How would she teach children who would much rather play?

CHAPTER TWENTY

A Troublemaker

$\mathcal{N}$essa's second day of school in Prairie River turned out to be her first day as a teacher.

In the morning, she dressed carefully with special attention to her hair. She wanted to wear it up on her head like Miss Eva, but did not have enough practice doing so. Her hair was thick and wavy. Her arms grew tired trying to twirl it up and pin it into place.

After half an hour of dropped hairpins, Nessa decided to wear one braid down her back. A tiny mirror above her bureau reflected her blue eyes and high cheekbones. A natural blush made her look healthy. She wondered if her mother had looked the same at her age.

Before going downstairs to help with breakfast, Nessa sat on the end of her bed and gazed out the window toward the sunrise, still just a hint of pink in the light blue sky.

Dear Jesus . . . thank You for this pretty day. . . . Here I am again, asking for You to guide me. . . . I don't know how to teach or what to do about Big Howard. . . . Miss Eva said it's the power of Your Holy Spirit that gives us courage and wisdom and, oh, how I need that now, Lord. . . . Thank You, amen.

The schoolroom looked as it had four days before except there were big chunks of mud where Howard had marched around the desks. He seemed pleased that his shoes tracked in such thick prints.

"Good morning, class," she said. "My name is Miss Vanessa. How is everyone today?" She smiled at Peter and Minnie in the front row, Augusta and Lucy in the second, Big Howard in the third, and Rolly in back. All of their feet were soaked or muddy from walking in the grass.

"Augusta, did your mother have her baby?"

"Nope — maybe it'll get born today — but Mama said I have to come to school, anyways."

All but Howard returned Nessa's friendly greeting. While she was asking the others how they were, he opened up his dinner pail and began eating a meat sandwich. He made smacking noises with his mouth and let the juice drip down his chin.

"Aaaaah!" he said, loud enough so those in front of him turned around in their seats.

A moment of panic fluttered in Nessa's chest until she remembered something Rolly had carried to school that morning. She walked to the last row, whispered something to him, then waited while he dug in his pocket.

He handed her his penknife.

"Thank you, Rolly," she said. "And thank you, Howard." As she passed his desk on the way back to the front, she picked up his pail and the sandwich that had been wrapped in a handkerchief. Howard's arm lashed out after her, but Nessa had already turned away.

At her desk, she spread everything out as if it were a picnic and began slicing the sandwich into six equal parts.

"Hey," he shouted, "you can't do that!"

Nessa answered, "Any student who eats during class will share with the others."

Howard slumped in his seat. He crossed his arms and scowled.

Nessa now distributed the pieces to the children, giving Howard his portion last. She did not plan on whipping anyone as Mr. Carey had done, but she understood that hunger had a way of making a person think twice about things.

Howard's dinner pail also held a large piece of chocolate cake with creamy white frosting. This, too, she divided and gave out.

"Now class will begin," she said.

It was nine o'clock. She pulled back the cloth from a basket Mrs. Lockett had given her and took out her Bible. A small piece of paper fluttered to the floor. When Nessa bent down to pick it up, she recognized Mrs. Lockett's handwriting, the same she'd seen on her recipes.

Dear Nessa,
This is for you: Ephesians, Chapter 3, Verses 17 through 20. You are in my prayers today.

Nessa thumbed through the pages until she found the passage. She wasn't sure how to go about teaching, but at least she could start each morning as Miss Eva had, by reading to her students from the Bible. Mrs. Lockett's verse was a good place to begin.

"That Christ may dwell in your hearts by faith; that ye, being rooted and grounded in love,

May be able to comprehend with all saints what is the breadth, and length, and depth, and height;

And to know the love of Christ, which passeth knowledge, that ye might be filled with all the fulness of God.

Now unto Him that is able to do exceeding abundantly above all that we ask or think, according to the power that worketh in us . . ."

Nessa looked up. A warm sensation filled her, a tenderness for her students, a strength. She felt with certainty that God had just spoken to her through His Word, that He had answered her prayer of that morning. He was encouraging her. Silently, she prayed, *God, thank You again for Mrs. Lockett. . . . Please bless her today.*

The *McGuffey Eclectic Reader* was what Nessa had used in Miss Eva's classroom. There were none in Prairie River because when the other teacher was murdered, the Cooley Boys stole all his materials. As soon as another supply wagon arrived, the sutler's store would be able to sell them to her students, along with slates, chalk, pencils, and paper. But meanwhile, without these things, Nessa was forced to make up lessons as she went along.

First, she drilled them on multiplication tables she knew by heart. Then she had a spelling bee where they spelled their own names and those of their family members. When the younger children started fidgeting, she remembered what Miss Eva had done. Nessa made everyone stand up and do ten jumping jacks, herself included. She'd forgotten how good it felt to stretch and jump.

Back in their seats again, they sang the "Alphabet Song," "Yankee Doodle," and "Oh! Susanna." Poetry was next. She read to them from Rolly's copy of Walt Whitman's *Leaves of Grass*. For a writing exercise, she would have them compose their own poems — even the littlest children could do this.

During a recitation, Howard rolled a twig along his desk by pushing it with his nose. When it dropped to the floor, he made a noisy production of crawling around to look for it. Three times he did this.

Nessa ignored him.

But when he began drumming his hands on his desk and whistling she said, "Howard, you're disturbing the class. Please stop it."

"I don't have to listen to you," he said. "My pa says you're nothing but an orphan. We don't know where in tarnation you come from or who your folks were."

Nessa drew in a breath. Suddenly, she no longer felt loving. Why was it that earlier she had felt so hopeful, but now she was just plain mad?

She did not like this boy one bit, and if she were not the teacher, she would have stormed over to his desk and slapped his face. That is what she *felt* like doing. Instead, she tried to calm her breathing and said a prayer in her head. It was three words: *Dear Jesus . . . help!*

She hoped her anger didn't show because she did not want to be a bad example to the children, but she felt color rise to her cheeks. She wondered what Miss Eva would do, but then remembered there were few problems in the orphanage with unruly students. That was because everyone knew Mr. Carey was downstairs and would be called in. By now, he would have whipped Howard for being lazy and disrespectful.

Nessa's eyes fell on something leaning in the corner against the wood box.

A shovel.

"Howard," she said, her voice calm, "have you ever dug for treasure?"

He looked at her in surprise, then shook his head.

"Well," she said, "there is treasure on the other side of this creek, and I need someone strong to start digging."

Howard sat up in his seat. "What kind of treasure?" he asked.

"It will take some time, but I promise you it will be beautiful."

"Where do I go?"

At this, Nessa looked out the window and saw the sun was nearly overhead. She was hungry and thought everyone else might be, too.

"Children," she said, "you may be dismissed for lunch. During recess, we'll take a walk. Howard will be the leader."

Augusta and Lucy hurried out in the sunshine with their dinner pails, followed by Minnie, Peter, and Rolly.

Big Howard got out of his seat and shuffled toward the door. He cast a sideways glance at Nessa as if to remind her that she'd taken away his food.

Peter had stayed behind and was waiting outside for him. A breeze rustled the grass around his knees and blew his hair about his shoulders. Windswept clouds streaked across the sky.

He handed Howard a chunk of bread that was buttered inside and thick with bacon. "Come on," said Peter. "Reckon I got enough for both of us."

CHAPTER TWENTY-ONE

Nessa's Garden

The next day, Nessa began class by reading Psalm 1 and Proverbs 1 to her students. Howard again brought out his dinner pail, removed the lid with a noisy clatter, but this time did not eat. Eventually, he snapped the lid back in place and put the pail under his seat.

After noon recess, Nessa led her students across the creek where large flat rocks served as stepping-stones. Willows cast deep shade. At their approach, a yellow mud turtle slid from the bank into the water. Its hind feet left claw marks in the sand.

Howard marched in front, carrying the shovel over his shoulder, followed by Rolly, who had brought his own shovel from home.

Yesterday, the children had marked off an area by walking through the grass single file, until a square had been formed, the size of a quarter-acre. Nessa directed them to count their steps, then add in their heads the distances so they would learn the mathematics. Next, she asked Howard to start digging at one of the corners, turning over the soil, working his way toward the center.

She put Rolly at the opposite corner and told them that when they met each other in the middle to then each dig toward another corner.

Howard didn't question this odd way of looking for treasure, nor how Miss Vanessa knew they should dig in this area. Rather, he was intent on being faster than Rolly and was elated not to be sitting in the classroom. He didn't yet see that he was helping to make a garden. The children carried every stone they uncovered to the edges so that soon the perimeter was rimmed with rocks.

By the end of Nessa's first week, each child had discovered something of interest. A bird's nest, the skull of a rabbit, and Indian arrowheads. They picked up a mummified lizard and the shed skin of a rattlesnake. Howard found one blue bead with part of a leather string through its center.

After two hours of being outside, Nessa led her students back into class. The room had the wonderful aroma of fresh air that clung to their hair and clothing. She asked them to report on the types of birds they saw fluttering up out of the grass, the insects, and the sounds and smells. Howard refused to participate in the discussions, but did not make trouble. On his desk was his blue bead that he kept picking up to roll between his fingers. He seemed willing to endure being inside in order to be part of the outdoor activities.

When Nessa walked home that Friday afternoon, she realized something. As fast and hard as the boys were digging, she was going to need help. Every inch of a garden must be turned over to reveal the soft soil. If they were to see beautiful flowers and vegetables by summer, they would need to plant soon.

Before supper, she went to the dry goods store. Mrs. Applewood was behind the counter, measuring wheat into five-pound sacks.

"Hello, Mrs. Applewood." She was careful not to say "Apple*worm*," though she secretly thought the name more fitting.

"Well, look who's here," said the woman, "the orphan who stole the teaching position from the properly bred Miss Laura — I told you to keep your hands to yourself." She pushed Nessa's fingers off a stout jar of candy that she was admiring.

Nessa flushed with embarrassment. People in the store turned to look at her. *I didn't steal anything!* she wanted to shout. She held back the urge to argue with Mrs. Applewood.

In a steady voice she said, "Good-bye then, madam. I'll take my business to the other sutler."

Though she felt like crying, Nessa held her head up as she walked to the door, ignoring the scowls and stares of other customers. She walked to the newspaper office. When Mr. Button saw her, his mustache lifted with his smile. He was untying his black printing apron.

"Why, Nessa," he said, "how nice to see you. I just put the kettle on for tea. Do you care to join me?"

"Yes, thank you."

A small black stove no taller than his knees radiated a pleasant warmth. It was just big enough to hold his teakettle on top. The stovepipe poked through the wall of the next room, where she could see that he was drying a pair of socks and a shirt over its warm stem. A cot with a mussed-up blanket showed where he had slept last night after staying up late to set type.

While they waited for the water to boil, Nessa described her first week of teaching.

"Do you know someone with a plow who would help with our garden?" she asked. "I'd like to plant by Monday."

"Hmm," said Mr. Button. He put a bowl of sugar on his workbench and arranged two cups with saucers. "Hmm," he said again, now chewing on a tip of his mustache. "I just might be able to accommodate you, young lady — anything else the school might need?"

Nessa sat up straight. "Why, yes, sir. There is something."

CHAPTER TWENTY-TWO

Church Picnic

Sunday was Nessa's first time in church since Palm Sunday, several weeks earlier. She was proud that her little schoolroom was neat and tidy as she had swept the floor and dusted the windowsills and desks. The men arranged the benches in rows so there was room for nearly thirty people. Miss Vanessa's desk had been pushed against a wall where it now held bowls and platters of food to be served later. They were covered with brightly colored cloths to keep away the flies.

The room was crowded. She recognized several people from her walks through town and was happy to see Fanny Jo and Laura. All the children were there. Peter had come with his aunt because his father was on duty and his mother was home ill. He sat beside Nessa so he could show her a caterpillar he found.

From their bench, she could look out a window across the creek. A swell of land dipped down, then rose to reveal a small clearing. On it was a square of newly plowed garden, finished yesterday by two Swedish farmers who had come into town for supplies. Nessa was grateful to Mr. Button, who had arranged everything.

She couldn't wait until tomorrow. She had so much to show her students.

The service lasted all morning, led by Reverend Ames, who had just arrived in town. He would be staying at Mrs. Lockett's boardinghouse this month until another minister replaced him. Then that man would stay a few weeks, with Mr. Ames returning the following month. When Nessa heard Reverend Ames explain that churches farther east planned to send their preachers here on a rotating basis, she drew in a sharp breath.

What if Reverend McDuff showed up? Even if Miss Eva and Albert told no one of her whereabouts, the man at the stage depot knew she had purchased a ticket for Prairie River.

This thought bothered her so much she was unable to concentrate on the sermon. When the congregation stood to sing the closing hymn, Nessa just stared out the window.

As everyone filed out of church, a wagon pulled up, driven by Mr. Applewood, his wife at his side. She wore a crisp new sunbonnet and he a black string tie. They smiled and waved to friends, but when they saw Nessa they turned away. She overheard that they had missed services because Mrs. Applewood couldn't decide which dress to wear.

Men helped unload the wagon and soon tables were

set up, made from planks laid over sawhorses. Benches were carried outside from the classroom. Mrs. Lockett flew into action with Mrs. Bell and the other ladies who brought out their covered dishes and arranged them on the tables. From picnic baskets, women pulled out plates, spoons, cups, and tablecloths. Boys filled the water pitchers from the creek.

Nessa wanted to help make things look pretty so she waded through the grass, picking daisies, buttercups, and tiny red roses. When a bouquet filled her arms, she put it in a pail of water for the largest table. A woman sitting there spread her skirt across the bench and, looking up at Nessa with a smile, said, "You can't sit here. It's for the officers' families."

"Oh," said Nessa, "I was just —"

"Never mind — shoo . . ." The woman waved her hand as if brushing off a fly.

A lump rose in Nessa's throat. She looked at the woman's pretty face and the smile that she had mistaken for friendliness. She noticed Peter and his friend on the other side of the table.

"I . . ." She wanted to say something, but turned away, hoping no one had seen the rebuke. To keep herself from tears, Nessa turned away and tried to sight the faraway flag.

She looked toward the fort but saw only wisps of smoke from someone's chimney. Around her in every direction, the grass had begun to turn from green to gold, miles of flat land stretching to the horizon without a fence or tree in sight. Just the riverbanks had timber.

Though enchanted by the beauty, she couldn't stop thinking how that woman didn't even want Nessa near her.

A hush over the group indicated Reverend Ames was praying for the meal — and it was a long one. Nessa glanced at the couples holding hands and the children leaning into their parents and felt a tear slide down her cheek. By the time everyone said amen, she had dried it with her sleeve and was mustering a brave smile.

She noticed Fanny Jo and Laura carrying their food to a table. Nessa wanted to sit with them, but worried they, too, might make her leave. When they called out her name to join them, relief swept over her.

"I'm glad to see you," Nessa told them. "Are you well?"

The sisters were more cheerful than the day she visited them at Suds Row. There was color in their cheeks and wisps from their upswept hair drifted about their faces. They looked trim and elegant in corseted dresses, as if they hadn't a care in the world.

Fanny Jo leaned over the table to whisper. "We've been helping the baker, to pay for our room. His wife died last month so we cook his supper, do laundry, and such."

Nessa wanted to ask about her lieutenant, but did not want to embarrass them or risk someone overhearing their conversation. Instead she said, "Would you like to come with me this afternoon to see Mrs. Bell's new house?" Nessa motioned to the next table, so the sisters would recognize Mrs. Bell. "The house is near the creek, not far from here. Rolly took all her things over in the wagon this morning before church."

"Oh, yes," said Laura. "I love Sunday visits — it reminds me of home — doesn't it you, Fanny Jo?"

Fanny Jo stared at her plate for a moment, then folded her napkin under its rim. She turned on the bench and delicately swung her legs over without her dress rising up. "Time to serve pie," she said. "Maybe the ladies need my help." Nessa thought perhaps Fanny Jo hadn't heard her sister.

A sudden cloud passed over the sun, darkening the sky. It was marbled with a black bottom. More clouds were behind it, dark gray and soaring toward them from the north. In unison, everyone looked up and immediately began gathering food and dishes into their baskets. A tablecloth — blue-and-white checked — flew off one of the tables and floated up into the air.

A crack of lightning split the clouds, then another. Thunder boomed like a cannon. Nessa felt nervous, not knowing what to do. For an instant, she fretted about the children, but remembered they were with their parents. She turned her attention to Mrs. Bell, who was holding her side and seemed out of breath. Her face was pale.

"Mrs. Bell," Nessa shouted above the wind, "are you all right?" She ushered her toward the schoolhouse, both of them bent over, unable to avoid the pelting rain.

She glanced behind her. Families were hurrying away in their wagons, heading for town. Colored cloths swirled in the air like leaves. In the confusion, she lost sight of Mrs. Lockett. Where were Rolly and Minnie?

By the time she helped Mrs. Bell into the doorway, their hair was soaked. Nessa noticed Fanny Jo was inside, kneeling beside young Peter, who was crying for his mother.

"You're all right, honey," she was saying to him. "Everything's going to be just fine. . . ." Laura was there, too, smoothing the boy's wet hair.

The wind howled and rattled windows. Rain seeped over the sills and dripped mud onto the floor. Nessa could see nothing outside except for gray. Suddenly, there was a groan unlike any she had ever heard. She turned to see Mrs. Bell leaning against the wall, sinking to her knees.

"Girls . . ." she said, trying to catch her breath, "it's time. . . ."

Nessa then understood that Mrs. Bell was about to have her baby.

CHAPTER TWENTY-THREE

After the Storm

The sisters and Nessa unbuttoned their skirts and stepped out of them, spreading them on the floor to make a bed in the corner. The cloth was wet from the rain but it was the best they could do. Clad only in petticoats, they helped Mrs. Bell out of her own dress, which they draped over her like a blanket.

When Peter saw her lying on the floor, he started to cry again. Nessa distracted him by asking him to help start a fire in the stove. She let him strike a match against the iron top, then drop it into the kindling and chips.

"You're in charge of the fire, Peter," said Nessa. She held his shoulders and gave him a smile of encouragement. "We need you to keep it going."

Lightning flashed at the windows, followed seconds later by thunder. The noise of the storm was deafening. It frightened Nessa, but she was more worried about the task ahead.

Fanny Jo said, "Mrs. Bell? Is this your first baby?"

". . . fourth . . ."

The sisters smiled with relief. "Then you know what to do, yes?" Laura asked.

The large woman rolled on her side, panting. The braids on her head had come unpinned and were now coiled on the floor by her neck. "My other three . . ." A long moment passed, then she closed her eyes. "At each birth, there were problems — they died before I could hold them — three years in a row. . . ."

Laura and Fanny Jo exchanged looks.

Nessa went to Peter, who was blowing on the tiny flame to help it catch. His shirt was soaked and he was shivering. "You're a good boy," she said, rubbing his arms for warmth. "And brave, too. The other day I saw how you kept your little sister from stepping on the ant-hill, remember? Do you think you can be brave again, Peter?"

Slowly, he nodded.

"All right, then," she continued, "Mrs. Bell's going to have a baby here and she needs you to pray for her. Can you do that?"

"Oh, yes, Miss Vanessa."

After an hour, the thunder and lightning passed, but it was still raining. The wind was fierce.

Nessa suggested one of them run for the surgeon who was treating a cholera outbreak at the fort. But the afternoon sky was so dark they couldn't make out any of the buildings in the distance. The sisters feared getting lost along the way and if they strayed from the path, they might miss the town altogether, wandering off onto the wide prairie. It could be dangerous to leave.

Nessa wanted to pray but was too worried to think quiet thoughts. Then she remembered part of Reverend Ames's sermon that morning. Not the exact words, but the truth of the matter.

Kneeling beside Mrs. Bell, Nessa bent close to her ear. "Mrs. Bell," she said, "please don't be afraid. Jesus made the lame walk and He gave sight to the blind. He healed anyone who asked Him, so I'm asking Him to help you — He can give you strength right now and He can keep your baby alive, I just know it. Peter's praying, too, see him over there by the stove?"

The woman grabbed Nessa's hand and squeezed it.

Fanny Jo lit a lantern with a match from the wood box. Light filled the glass chimney, then spread throughout the room. A bucket of water was heating on the stove, brought in by Peter from the rain barrel outside.

The wind had dropped to a breeze so Nessa opened the door for fresh air and stood on the step. The sky was low with black clouds. The remains of the sunset drew a golden streak of light along the western horizon. *It must be close to six o'clock,* she thought. Soon they would be able to see lights from town, and one of them could go fetch a wagon.

The sound of a soft voice singing drew her attention inside.

Mrs. Bell was cradling her son, Oliver, in her arms. She gazed at his face and caressed the tiny pink hand that was curled around her finger. Her song was a hymn of thanksgiving.

The sisters had each removed one of their petticoats and torn them into strips of cloth to bathe the infant and Mrs. Bell. The schoolroom was cozy with lamplight and a warm glow from the stove. Nessa felt an ache in her chest as she watched the baby.

She still couldn't believe what she had just witnessed. One moment, Mrs. Bell was lying on the floor, laboring. Then the next, Fanny Jo handed Nessa a wet, squirming newborn no bigger than a doll. It was a miracle. She could feel the life in him, the warmth. His eyes squinted out of a puffy red face and gazed at her. Nessa loved him instantly. The sisters wrapped him — cooing and exclaiming how beautiful he was — then placed him in Mrs. Bell's outstretched arms.

Nessa wondered if her own mother had held her so tenderly. After some minutes, she decided yes, she was sure of it. Without understanding how she knew this, she was certain her mother had loved her.

And now, more than ever, Nessa was thankful she had not married Reverend McDuff.

Nessa stepped outside to breathe in the aroma of sage-brush and moist earth when she noticed a figure in the distance, coming from town.

It was a woman, walking fast, carrying a lantern that cast speckled light around her path. Over her other arm was a basket.

Soon enough, Nessa realized it was Mrs. Lockett.

Nessa ran through the wet grass to greet her and help with the basket, which was full of sandwiches and a jar of milk.

"Honey," cried Mrs. Lockett, "I've been worryin' and prayin' where you might be and, finally, I felt like the Lord was nudging me to come this-a way. Thank God you're all right — that was some storm, wasn't it?"

At the sound of a new voice, Peter ran outside. Even though Mrs. Lockett wasn't his mother, he threw himself into her wide skirt and held on until she was able to set down her lantern and pull him into her arms.

"There, there, Peter," she said. "Everything's all right now." To Nessa she said, "His ma got outta her sickbed to come lookin' for him and was panicked, but I told her more'n likely you two were together and not to worry. Told her that you would care for Peter like he was your own little boy."

At this, Peter slipped his hand in Nessa's and leaned against his teacher.

Mrs. Lockett patted Nessa's cheek. Then she picked up her lantern and headed for the schoolhouse where yellow light filled the doorway.

When she saw her friend Mrs. Bell nursing her new baby, a sob caught in her voice.

"Oh, Lord Jesus, thank you," she said. "Thank you so much."

CHAPTER TWENTY-FOUR

―――――◆―――――

Overflowing

$\mathfrak{M}$onday brought blue skies and the sweet scent of grass and soil washed by rain. The garden was muddy, so Miss Vanessa instructed her students to first remove their shoes. With the help of Mrs. Lockett — who was respected by even the officers' wives — Nessa had gathered sunflower and cucumber and pumpkin seeds from different folks in town.

She knew little about gardening but did remember following Miss Eva around the vegetable patch at the orphanage when she was younger. Something always seemed to grow under Miss Eva's care.

Most of the women in Prairie River had brought packets of seeds from their previous homes, saved in squares of paper folded several times over so they wouldn't spill out. Several of them shared with the new teacher, and their generosity made up for those who had politely declined to donate. Nessa quickly forgot the names and descriptions and colors they told her, and couldn't recall which was a vegetable or which was a flower. Everything was all mixed up by the time she put them in a basket and carried it to school.

Planting took all afternoon.

Because Rolly and Howard were the biggest boys, they each filled a pail at the creek and carried it to the garden. The younger children then took turns using the dipper and a cup to water the rows. It was hard work, but Nessa used the time to point out a red-winged blackbird, then a hawk soaring overhead. She asked them to describe the beetles and grasshoppers moving over the dirt, and the worms they uncovered.

When the buckets were half full and not so heavy, Rolly and Howard carried them along the rows, dribbling water over the thumbprints made by the children from pressing down the dirt.

Nessa walked backward to admire their parcel of earth, the golden prairie grass brushing against her skirt. "It's perfect!" she said. "I'm so proud of everyone. Now we'll just wait and see what happens."

At the creek, they sat on rocks to wash the mud from their feet. The water shimmered in the late afternoon light and a breeze stirred the willows overhead. To Nessa, it was the most beautiful day since she came to Prairie River.

Overcome with emotion, she blinked back tears. To have witnessed Mrs. Bell struggle in childbirth, then to see the joy on her face when she held her baby was something she would never forget. And on top of everything, Nessa was encouraged by the way her students worked together without arguments. She wanted to jump or yell or do something to show her happiness, but she was the teacher and must be disciplined. With a growing affection for the children, she watched Augusta and Lucy swish their feet in the creek. Minnie was helping Peter tie his shoes. Rolly was skipping a rock downstream that looked like a small brown frog hopping over the water.

Big Howard sat by himself. He had taken the blue bead from his pocket and held it up to the sunlight. When he saw Nessa watching him he turned away, but then a moment later he shyly returned her smile.

Late that evening when the house was still, Nessa slipped from the kitchen to the back porch where her shawl hung on a nail. She put it around her shoulders, then walked outside. The air was cool and smelled sweet from the lavender bushes that lined the path. Overhead, a canopy of stars glistened against the black sky. From the corner of her eye she saw a streak of light — a shooting star — then another over the horizon. The beauty of the night took her breath away.

She could hear crickets and, from the vast prairie, the *yip-yip-yip* of coyotes. In the distance, a wolf howled. Nessa was startled by noises coming from the creek — splashing and a *whoosh* as if someone let out a deep sigh. In the starlight, she noticed an immense shadow moving along the bottomland, but it was some moments before she realized what it was: a herd of buffalo coming to drink.

I wish Albert were here to see all of this, she thought.

Nessa's heart was overflowing. In her room, she opened a window for the breeze, then climbed into bed. Pulling her fur robe up to her cheek, she wanted to thank God for everything, but drifted to sleep before the words came.

CHAPTER TWENTY-FIVE

◆━━◆◆◆━━◆

The Soddy

The schoolroom was filled with morning light when the children took their seats. Nessa stood in front, her dress freshly starched and ironed. She was pleased with herself because she had two surprises.

Also, she was excited because she had tried something new with her hair. Like Mrs. Bell, she brushed it into braids, then coiled them atop her head. The hairpins were poked in at various angles, making her scalp ache, but she was glad to finally look like a lady.

"Here is my first surprise, boys and girls. . . ." Nessa held her hands behind her back. "Lucy, you pick first."

The girl pointed to Nessa's right arm. Nessa fiddled for a moment, then handed Lucy a new pencil, four inches long. She did this for each student except Howard because he rolled his eyes at this game. His, she gently put on his desk.

Nessa explained she had visited the carpenter's shop and bought three pencils. He sawed them in half so the six students could each have one. She didn't mention the cost was a penny a piece or that she had paid for them with her own money.

"Now, the best part," she said. From her basket, she pulled out six sheets of brown paper. They were blank on one side with last week's news printed on the other. Folded in half, they were like little books with something to read on the outside and a place to write on the inside.

"This way we can practice reading *and* penmanship," Nessa said. "Mr. Button told me with each issue of his newspaper he'll save a few sheets for us, then we'll . . ."

Giggling interrupted her. Augusta clapped her hand over her mouth and looked away, but Lucy was laughing, too.

"Yes, girls?" asked Nessa. "Is there something you wish to say?"

Minnie was swinging her feet under her desk. She bit her lip to keep from laughing but did not answer her teacher.

"Minnie, what is it?" Nessa asked again.

Minnie shook her head, still unwilling to respond.

Finally, Big Howard pointed to her. "Your hair . . . it looks like you slept in a barn."

Nessa touched her head and realized one braid had slid down above her ear and the other was completely unraveled. She was embarrassed beyond words. Her plan to look like a lady had failed.

She wanted to dismiss class immediately, but knew the children would tell their parents. She did not want the townspeople to think she was a coward.

"Well, then," she said after a long silence. "I reckon we must carry on with things, yes, class?"

While she dictated vocabulary for them to write on their papers, she combed her fingers through her hair and made one thick braid. Using a piece of string from her basket she tied a knot on the end and thought, *It is too hard to be fancy, anyway.*

Every day during noon recess, Nessa and her students walked across the creek, filled the pails, then watered their garden. Peter tried to carry his own bucket, but half the water always sloshed out along the path. Nessa smiled at this.

The days grew warmer and soon the dirt patch took on a light green hue. Things were growing! To Nessa, it was a beautiful sight. She had no idea of what would come up, or where, but she was certain it would be lovely.

One Sunday, Mrs. Bell came to church with her husband and little Oliver. Her complexion was rosy and she looked about half the size she did before giving birth.

"May I hold him?" Nessa whispered.

Mrs. Bell slid the bundled baby onto Nessa's lap. The tiny face was the same that looked up at her when he was just one minute old, but now his eyes were wide open as he smiled at her. Nessa touched her nose to his then gave him back to his mother because he was soaking wet and now so were her sleeves.

During the congregation's dinner afterward, Mrs. Bell invited Nessa and Minnie to ride home with them.

The road was alongside the creek. In a swell of land, Mr. Bell pulled the horses to a stop, then helped his wife from the wagon. There was no house or barn in sight, just open prairie.

Minnie took Nessa's hand for comfort. "Where are we?" she whispered.

Mrs. Bell smiled. She pointed to what looked like a stick poking up from the ground.

"There's our chimney," she said. "Come." With her baby in the crook of her arm, she led the girls along a path that dipped down and around a low hill. Stepping on a footbridge, they crossed a stream where there was a cluster of wild plum trees. Then Mrs. Bell pointed behind them to an embankment.

To Nessa's surprise there was a door in the side of this hill with a window on each side.

"Is this your house?" she asked.

"Why, yes," answered Mrs. Bell, "it's a dugout — a soddy. Since most of the lumber coming to these parts is for Fort Larned, we figured we'd make do this way. Lots of folks are. Our barn, too. Henry's taking the horses there now. Do come in."

It took some minutes for Nessa's eyes to adjust to the dim light.

They stood in a cozy room the size of Mrs. Lockett's kitchen. A bed was in one corner with a quilt smoothed over it, a cradle at the foot. Against one wall was an iron cooking stove with two chairs and a table, which was covered with a cheerful red cloth, a tin can filled with white daisies in its center. Wood beams overhead had pans, pots, and other utensils hanging from nails. Between these beams, the ceiling was dirt, with bits of grass and roots dangling down, as if they were underground in a bear's den. It was more rugged than the schoolhouse, but it was tidy.

Mr. Bell came in with his rifle, holding up a large jackrabbit by its hind feet.

"Will you girls stay for supper now?" he asked. "We'd be mighty glad for your company."

"Yes, thank you," said Nessa as Minnie nodded in agreement. Mrs. Lockett had already given them permission to stay if invited.

They both set to work to help Mrs. Bell. Minnie peeled potatoes and Nessa fetched water from the creek to set on the stove. Mrs. Bell sat on her bed to nurse Oliver, a blanket draped over her shoulder.

"I'm grateful to you both," she began, then in a suddenly low and measured voice she said, "Nessa . . . do . . . not . . . move. . . . Stay . . . right . . . where . . . you . . . are. . . ."

Nessa had been stirring the kettle, her back to Mrs. Bell. The spoon she was holding stopped midair. She saw Minnie staring at her, eyes wide.

She heard a drip from the spoon fall into the kettle.

The next sound was a hiss. Nessa could see Mrs. Bell lowering the baby into the cradle, and then quickly grasping a handle. With one swoop, her arm knocked something to the earthen floor with a skillet.

Clumps of dirt fell from the ceiling where the pan had scraped it. Dirt sprinkled down Nessa's neck and inside her dress, but she was too frightened to shake herself off. Standing perfectly still, her eyes looked downward.

A black snake with a yellow stripe down its back slithered toward her. It was about four feet long.

With another blow, Mrs. Bell rushed at the floor and killed it.

Then Minnie burst out, "Oh, Nessa, it was crawling for your head — down from the rafter — I saw its long tongue. . . ." Minnie rushed to put her arms around her waist and clung to her.

Nessa felt faint. She lowered herself onto a chair and pulled Minnie into her lap. The girl's blond pigtails were mussed and there were tears on her cheeks. Nessa held her close.

Mrs. Bell swept the snake outside then flung it into the creek where it floated away. "That's one bother with a dugout," she said, returning the broom to a corner. "Critters fall from the ceiling on occasion."

CHAPTER TWENTY-SIX

<hr>

The Sutler's Daughter

On the way back to town, the girls walked along the high path above the creek. In the distance, they could see a cloud of dust rising above the Santa Fe Trail.

"Hurry!" Nessa said, grabbing Minnie's hand and starting to run. "That's the stage. . . . There could be mail." She prayed in her heart there would be a letter for Minnie and Rolly from their father, but didn't say so. She knew it had been two years since they had heard from him and Nessa didn't want to upset Minnie, but she hoped that there might be news now that the war was over. Nessa also hoped to receive mail of her own.

They arrived at the fort out of breath. The driver was on the roof of the coach, lowering a trunk to the ground. He recognized Nessa from last month and nodded in the direction of outlying buildings.

"Same as last time, young lady, mail's at the sutler's. But it's a new fella, arrived just this morning. He likely won't get it sorted till the wee hours. Name's Filmore."

"Thank you, sir," called Nessa as she headed with Minnie toward Officers' Row. The sidewalk was not as dusty as the path that ran along the parade ground so they stepped up onto it. She liked the sound their shoes made on the wood planks, for it reminded her of walking with Albert in a real town. Also, she liked passing the sod homes where there was often piano music and children playing.

"You there!" a man's voice called.

Nessa looked up. A soldier in the plain blue jacket of a private was pushing a wheelbarrow heaped with small sticks of firewood.

"Whose daughters are you?" he asked, setting down the handles to adjust his cap.

Nessa tried to think of an answer. Was he teasing or did he really want to know who their parents were?

In a soft voice Minnie said, "My daddy is Charlie Lockett, sir. He's a captain, gone to war."

"Didn't hear you, little sister. Speak up."

"Captain Charles Lockett," Nessa said for her.

The private pointed to the parade ground where rows of infantry were marching to the *rat-a-tat-tat* of a drum.

"The only captain at this post is out there drilling with his men, but his name ain't Lockett. This here walk is for families of real officers, not made-up ones. Now git, both of you — the path's over there."

Nessa swallowed the pain that made her throat ache. She drew herself up to her full height and, taking Minnie's hand, looked the private in the eye.

"We'll be on our way now," she said. But instead of getting off the sidewalk as he had ordered, she continued its entire length, enjoying the sound of their every step.

Most of all, she was pleased to have heard Minnie mention her father. And that they had been mistaken for sisters.

Nessa walked Minnie home, then went to the sutler's. It was nearing sunset and, as the soldiers were occupied elsewhere and the store was almost empty, she felt comfortable going inside. It was similar to the Applewoods', with shelves of cloth, rope, and other supplies, the good smell of spices and coffee.

Mr. Filmore was sorting the mail. His tiny office was behind the counter with a wall of cubbyholes.

"Hello," said Nessa. "Is it all right if I look around?"

"Yes, indeed," he said. He turned to regard her, then smiled. "Why, my daughter is about your age — Ivy!" he called. "Come out here, sweetheart."

The girl came from the next room. "Oh, hello!" she said when she saw Nessa.

Nessa liked her immediately. Ivy's brown hair was in two braids tied together behind her back with a wide red ribbon. Her dress was like Nessa's, gingham with some petticoat showing at the hem and revealing high-buttoned shoes that were scuffed.

Just then the front door opened. Nessa recognized the voice of Mrs. Applewood, shrill and unpleasant.

"Mr. Filmore," said the woman to the sutler, "since you folks are new to town, I gotta warn you about some of our less reputable citizens." She glanced at Nessa.

"My husband and I run the other store. We don't cotton to those who claim to be orphans and come from who-knows-where, and I would advise you to do the same. Good day to you, sir, and welcome to Prairie River." She turned on her heel and walked toward the door.

Nessa was stunned. Her heart started racing. She wanted to slap the woman. Something made her want to grab the tight little bun on top of Mrs. Applewood's head and yank it till her hair streamed in her face. But while Nessa thought of such revenge, she looked at Ivy. The girl's friendly smile was fading, and her father held his palms in the air, bewildered.

Without thinking, Nessa rushed to the door and blocked Mrs. Applewood's exit. All the hurt of recent days — the woman at the picnic and the soldier — made Nessa feel like exploding. She was too mad to stand still and too mad to pray, though the thought did flit into her mind.

"I'm — not — a bad person," she said. "But you, madam, are as mean as a goat and so is your husband."

Nessa looked at Ivy, then burst into tears. She ran home, ran upstairs, and threw herself on her bed. She didn't know anything about her parents, but believed with all her heart they had loved her and that she had been special to them. But now she did not feel the least bit special. Burying her face in her buffalo robe, she wept long into the night.

She didn't even hear Mrs. Lockett knock on her door.

CHAPTER TWENTY-SEVEN

Two Letters

Nessa woke with a bitter taste in her mouth and a heavy heart. She was ashamed of herself for calling Mrs. Applewood a goat. She felt humiliated to be treated as if she'd done something wrong, especially in front of people who didn't know her.

At the thought of Ivy, Nessa cried fresh tears. She hadn't realized until yesterday how much she yearned for a friend her own age. Ivy seemed like such a nice girl and her father was kind, too. Nessa was embarrassed they'd seen her lose her temper. She felt like staying in bed all day, but knew she couldn't. School started in an hour and she mustn't let the children down.

As she pulled her nightgown over her head, she noticed two letters on the floor by her bureau. She clutched them to her heart. It had taken only a moment to recognize the handwriting of her beloved Miss Eva on one envelope and the wobbly penmanship of Albert on the other. A fifty-cent postage stamp was on each one, in the upper right-hand corners.

She wanted to rip them open and read them immediately, but there would be no time to savor the words. There were still chores to be done, and Minnie was calling from downstairs that breakfast was ready.

At the table, Mrs. Lockett served her a bowl of oatmeal with brown sugar, cinnamon, and fresh cream. She patted Nessa's shoulder and smiled, but did not ask about her mail or why she had missed supper.

All morning, Nessa stood before her students, aware that the letters were inside her left sleeve. She could feel the paper crinkle against her skin. During her walk to school through the wet grass, she had planned ahead to the noon recess when she would sit by the creek, open the envelopes, then read.

But her plan was interrupted.

Ivy had come to school and was sitting in the back row beside Rolly. She politely said, "Good morning, Miss Vanessa," with the other children, as if it didn't bother her to be taught by someone her age. Her smile told Nessa she wanted to be friends.

At noon, they sat together on a rock in the center of the creek, watching the children play tag along the bank. Nessa learned Ivy's mother and two sisters had died last year of cholera. Her father wanted to start a new life in a new place without so many sad memories.

"Papa heard about Prairie River," she said. "It being on the trail at Fort Larned seemed a good place to run a business. Also, two of our friends came out before us and are working at the sutler's store down at Fort Dodge, so here we are. What about you?"

Nessa hesitated. She badly wanted to have a friend her own age. Ivy was cheerful and kind; she was wonderful, Nessa thought. But Nessa didn't want to tell about herself and didn't know where else to begin. If Ivy learned about the orphanage and that she had run away, others would find out and might think Nessa was untrustworthy.

"I'm sorry," Nessa said, standing. She pulled her dress to her knees so she could jump over the water to the embankment. "It's time for class."

At last, Nessa read Miss Eva's letter. She leaned into the lamplight, from her bench in the kitchen. Supper dishes were done and put away. Mrs. Lockett was kneading dough to set out to rise for tomorrow's bread. Minnie and Rolly were on the floor at the far end of the room playing marbles. Nessa liked it when it was just the four of them and guests were in the parlor or on the front porch visiting among themselves. She felt as if she had a real family.

All was well in Independence, Miss Eva wrote. Mary was learning to read the newspaper that Albert brought by every few days. The final paragraph stirred Nessa's curiosity and made her heart turn over.

Nessa dear, I found something that belongs to you. It apparently has been in the attic since the day you

were brought to us so long ago. As soon as I receive your written permission, I will send it to you on the next stage. Please send your response to Albert at the *Gazette*. He will then bring it to me.
Your loving,
Miss Eva

An understanding filled Nessa. Whatever this was, Miss Eva needed to keep it a secret from Mr. Carey. Sitting in the warmth of the kitchen, surrounded by the Locketts, Nessa looked up from reading. She was bursting to tell them this exciting news, but she wasn't sure what it meant.

Instead, she jumped up from the bench and put her arms around a surprised Mrs. Lockett and kissed her cheek. Then she hurried to the rolltop desk to write Miss Eva.

Later in her room, Nessa finally read Albert's letter.

Guess what. I tripped into a bucket of ink that was on the floor and knocked it over — it spilled and made a terrible mess — but the editor didn't whip me or nothing, said he knew it was an accident. I wish you could meet him, Nessa.

But Albert also wrote about something that sent chills up her spine. He had had an upsetting episode with Reverend McDuff: The preacher visited Albert on Easter morning, demanding to know where Nessa had gone because even Mr. Carey was searching.

He said he's going to find you, Nessa, if it's the last thing he does, on account that he thinks God said you're supposed to be *Mrs.* McDuff. Well, I told him that as long as I'm alive, there ain't gonna be a wedding between you two. He is busy praying that he finds you, but I am praying that he don't. Write again soon.

Albert

Nessa pressed the letter to her heart, then tucked it under her pillow with Miss Eva's so she could read them each night before going to sleep.

So many emotions filled her as she lay looking up at the dark ceiling. She was excited to think about what Miss Eva might be sending her. Maybe it was something about her parents or it would reveal her middle name. Then when her thoughts turned to Reverend McDuff, she felt sick at heart. What would she do if he came to Prairie River?

But then recalling Albert's words made her feel hopeful again. Knowing he fiercely did not want her to marry the preacher brought her unexpected joy.

Six weeks after Nessa became a teacher, the last day of school arrived. She planned a picnic with Rolly and Minnie's help. They drove the wagon with a hamper full of fried chicken, boiled eggs, pickles, and rolls with fresh butter. Also, there were jars of sarsaparilla sweetened with honey and ginger.

The children were excited to have a party, so everyone

dressed up. Howard had made a necklace from his blue bead and a thin strip of leather. He wore it over his shirt between his red suspenders. Though he still wouldn't participate in class discussions, Nessa admired the way he had led the children to the creek every afternoon, so they could water the garden.

"So," he said while everyone was eating. "Who's gonna come out here with me to help water now that there ain't no more school?"

Augusta raised her hand, then Lucy. They wore frilly white aprons over their homespuns, and white bows on the ends of their pigtails.

Peter yelled, "I will, I will!"

Rolly said, "We can use my wagon. . . . Me and Minnie'll come fetch you, Howard — and the rest of you, too."

Ivy sat on a blanket, her face shaded by her wide-brimmed bonnet. "I'll come, too — my sisters and I had a garden back home that was . . ."

When she turned away with tears, Nessa's heart melted. She wanted to touch Ivy's hand, to comfort her, and to be her best friend. To say that she understood her sorrow. But the children were watching and she didn't know how to put it all into words.

Nessa cleared her throat to keep back her own emotion.

"Ivy," she said, "please do come — we would love it if you would."

CHAPTER TWENTY-EIGHT

Indian Trouble

A week after the last day of school, Ivy ran into the yard of the boardinghouse. Her braids were undone, as if she'd been interrupted while brushing her hair.

Nessa was out back, hanging laundry on the clothesline. "What is it?" she asked Ivy.

"Such terrible news — Indians attacked Fort Dodge — they stole their horses and killed two sutlers."

Mrs. Lockett rushed out of the barn from milking the cow, and Ivy fell into her arms. "Honey, why are you so upset?" she asked.

Ivy started to cry. "Mrs. Lockett, those sutlers were our friends from back home. . . ."

"There, there. Sit down right here." She led Ivy to a bench by the garden and sat next to her, patting her hand.

"Papa knew them since boyhood, those two — he's devastated, they were his oldest friends — and what if the Indians come for him next? What'll I do without my father?"

"Honey, don't you go worryin' about what might never happen. Fort Larned here is bigger and better protected than at Dodge, and there's always plenty of soldiers on guard."

Nessa envied how Mrs. Lockett soothed Ivy with her wise words and kind voice. She wished she could be the one to comfort her. She reached into the basket and pulled up a bedsheet to hang, first snapping out the heavy wrinkles. Taking two clothespins from her apron pocket, she clipped it to the line.

She had grown fond of praying silently wherever she was, instead of waiting until going to bed at night. Miss Eva had taught her that God was always available.

Lord, she began, *why is it hard to make friends? Please help me be as loving as Mrs. Lockett. . . .* Nessa gazed out onto the prairie where clouds were building in the distance. *And also, since You created the Indians same as us and You love them the same, would You please show all of us how to be friends?* She took a deep breath and looked over at Ivy. *Thank You, Jesus, amen.*

After supper, Nessa sat on the back porch with Rolly. They were reading a book on sailing ships together, each taking turns with a page. Mrs. Lockett appeared from the kitchen and lay an envelope in Nessa's lap.

"Mr. Applewood brought this by," she said. "It's your pay for six weeks as schoolteacher."

"Oh!" cried Nessa. She had forgotten that she was earning money while teaching. Though it had been one of her reasons for wanting the job in the first place, she became attached to the children — even Big Howard — and had put her mind to caring for them.

She looked in the envelope. Thirteen dollars and fifty cents! It was a fortune, and she had earned it on her own. In her next letter to Miss Eva, she would send two more dollars to help pay off her debt.

"Come on, Rolly," she said, pulling him up off the seat. "Let's find Minnie and explore the sutler's. I'm buying chocolates or taffy or whatever you like, and something for your mother, too. I'm rich!"

Summer was suddenly upon them. The windows in the house were open for fresh air and to coax in a breeze when one arose.

Nessa missed the trees and rain of Missouri, but she had grown to love the wide-open prairie and the big sky that seemed to change hourly. Just when she thought it would be blue all day, a small white cloud would appear on a horizon. It would float overhead, then change shapes a dozen times before drifting off. When thunderclouds hid the sun, they boiled upward with a halo of light around their edges, then the wind would sweep them away. Even in a clear sky, there were birds soaring and flitting against a backdrop of blues, pinks, and golds, from dawn to sunset.

Every day was beautiful, Nessa decided, no matter what it looked like.

A hymn played in her head, from church last Sunday. She sang it to herself in her room, then when she was outside raking the henhouse, she sang some more. The words made her happy because they reflected her deep feelings for the prairie and for the Locketts.

For the beauty of the earth,
For the splendor of the skies,
For the love which from our birth
Over and around us lies —
Lord of all, to Thee we raise
This our hymn of grateful praise.

For the joy of human love,
Brother, sister, parent, child,
Friends on earth and friends above,
Pleasures pure and undefiled —
Lord of all, to Thee we raise
This our hymn of grateful praise.

One afternoon Peter knocked on the door of the boardinghouse and asked for Nessa. He carried a bird's nest he had found in the grass. It fit in his palm and was empty except for some pieces of blue eggshell.

"Look, Miss Vanessa," he said when she came out to the porch. "A magpie was poking at 'em. I chased it away but was too late. Do you think the babies were afraid?"

Nessa kneeled in front of him and brushed a lock of hair from his eyes. "That was brave of you, Peter. And if the babies were afraid it was over quickly, and they are safe in God's hands now. Would you like to come inside?"

He set the nest down on a ledge and followed her into the kitchen where cinnamon rolls were cooling by the open window.

"Want to help me?" she asked.

He nodded, preoccupied by wiggling his loose front tooth. She tied an apron around his neck and put a bowl on the table in front of him. Handing him a wooden spoon, she began pouring sugar into the bowl, then some milk and soft butter.

"Now, stir," she said.

Quickly, his arm grew tired, but he kept beating when she told him his reward.

"You get to lick the bowl. Keep going, Peter."

When the icing was smooth, much of it was splattered in his hair and on the table, but Nessa merely gave him a cloth to wipe his face. She was remembering when she, too, was six years old and Miss Eva had patiently showed her how to do things. She brought over the pans, then demonstrated to Peter how he should dribble the frosting on with a larger spoon.

Mrs. Lockett came into the kitchen while he was midway through his task. He was concentrating so hard he didn't hear them talking about what a splendid job he was doing. The rolls were as large as a man's fist and swirled with cinnamon and brown sugar. By the time he finished decorating them, Minnie was at the table watching and so was Rolly.

Peter looked up to find the four of them smiling at him.

CHAPTER TWENTY-NINE

———◆◇◆———

Independence Day

At dawn on the Fourth of July, a cannon blast from the fort awoke the citizens of Prairie River. In case anyone had forgotten, it was an important holiday: eighty-nine years since the signing of the Declaration of Independence.

To celebrate, a parade of children led their pet dogs, donkeys, and goats around the dusty, windblown square.

Peter carried his cat, both of them dressed like soldiers. The cat wore a little blue coat pulled over its paws and a miniature blue hat — a tricorn — fastened with a ribbon. Two holes were cut out of the top for its ears. The cat's mouth was open, revealing the tip of its pink tongue as it panted under the hot sun. Yellow Dog walked alongside them, a red kerchief around her neck.

Other children had also dressed their pets. Nessa had never seen so many animals in Revolutionary War costumes. The army band played "Yankee Doodle" and other patriotic songs — it was a fine assortment of trumpets, a bugle, drums, and a clarinet. The civilians and families lined the parade ground and applauded. Then came the soldiers, marching proudly in crisp uniforms, one of them carrying the Stars and Stripes. Nessa watched the sisters as they stood in front of the bakery, and thought how pretty they looked in their hoop skirts and corsets. She wondered if Fanny Jo's husband knew they hadn't gone home to Pennsylvania.

After the parade, Howard and some of the other children lit firecrackers. Unfortunately, the wind ignited the sparks, which spread into a small brushfire. A detail of men stomped out the flames while others passed buckets of water from the creek. The post commander decided the grass was too dry this year for any more fireworks.

While Nessa helped Mrs. Lockett carry their basket to the river where everyone would be picnicking, she asked why Mr. and Mrs. Applewood were so patriotic. They were handing out small flags to everyone and had unfurled a red-white-and-blue banner from the roof of their store.

"And another thing," said Nessa, "they're not friendly to you or Rolly or Minnie. . . . How come you're nice to them?" Though this changed the subject, she had wanted to ask this question for some time.

"It may seem odd," answered Mrs. Lockett, "but their great-grandfathers and mine knew each other. They fought together in the War of Independence. Somehow our common history makes it easier to say howdy-do. But the truth is, my dear, I've just plain decided to get along with folks, whether I like 'em or not."

Nessa looked at Mrs. Lockett's kind face and her hair combed neatly atop her head, her bonnet hanging down her back. She imagined her mother would have been as pretty and nice. The blanket they were sitting on felt like a small island in a sea of grass, as if they could talk forever without anyone hearing them. Nessa wanted to ask about her husband, if there was some way people could look for him in hospitals, but she didn't want to upset her.

Children's voices distracted her. "Miss Vanessa," called Lucy, "want to walk with us down by the creek where it ain't so hot?"

"And then we'll go see our garden?" said Augusta.

Nessa jumped up. "Why, yes, I'd love to," she said. She started to gather dirty plates into their basket, but Mrs. Lockett waved her off.

"Run along, dears. I'll take care of this."

Soon, Ivy had joined them, then Minnie, then Peter. When Big Howard saw where they were headed, he caught up to them with two extra pails for watering.

In the garden, they walked along the rows between green clumps of zucchini and vines with melons. Rising up like sentries in no particular order were sunflowers, their tall golden heads turned toward the sun. It was the most cheerful vegetable patch Nessa had ever seen.

The girls used their aprons to gather dandelion greens for tea and salads. In another month, they'd be able to pick squash and little cucumbers their mothers could use for making pickles.

Nessa had never felt happier. Every row had a colorful assortment of flowers and vegetables arranged haphazardly like a patchwork quilt. She was proud of her students and was going to tell them so when she noticed Howard looking off toward the open prairie, his hand shading his eyes. Nessa straightened her back and stood up, calling to him.

He didn't answer. She set down her armload of flowers and hurried toward him.

"I can't find Peter," he said.

Nessa whirled toward the garden. "Peter . . . Peter!" she cried.

The others looked up.

Rolly pointed. "I seen him chasin' magpies again — over there a-ways. . . ."

Nessa lifted the hem of her skirt and ran. Ivy followed with the littler girls.

"Peter!" they cried. "Where are you? Peter!"

The prairie was flat, but not really, for there were slopes and rolling grasses that hid depressions in the earth. He could be anywhere. They kept calling.

Nessa was frantic. Her heart raced as she cried out his name again and again. *Could Indians possibly have taken him? Please, no . . .*

"Maybe he went back to town," said Lucy. "Should we look there, Miss Vanessa?"

"Yes, that's a good idea, Lucy. Augusta, you and Minnie go with her and *stay together*. Do *not* stop until you reach the fort. See? There yonder is the flag. When you get there, yell for help. Now go, hurry!"

For twenty minutes they searched, fanning out in the high grass. Rolly, Howard, Nessa, and Ivy. They called Peter's name, then stood still. Finally, on the breeze came a faint voice. They listened. Nessa stood on her tiptoes, as if doing so would help her hear better.

The voice came again.

"Over there!" Howard ran into the wind. The others followed, racing until they came to a gulley that dipped down from the level ground.

There lay Peter. His face was ashen and he gasped for breath, trying not to cry.

Nessa knelt next to him and put his head in her lap. When she noticed his left hand she felt as if her heart might stop beating. It was swollen and blood was caked around two puncture wounds by his thumb. The skin had turned purplish black.

"Was it a snake, Peter?" She kept her voice calm.

He nodded.

"Did it have rattles?"

"Yes," he whispered. His lips were dry and there was a wheeze coming from his chest.

Oh, God . . . dear God. Nessa felt a cold emptiness in the pit of her stomach and struggled against panic. Bending down to the bite, she tried to suck out the poison, but only tasted blood.

Choking back the tears gathering in her throat, she said, "We're taking you home now, Peter. You're a brave lad. Your ma and pa will be proud of you."

She kissed the top of his head and breathed in the scent of his hair — sunshine and wind and little boy. Then she looked at Big Howard. Without a word passing between them, he lifted Peter into his arms and started running for town.

CHAPTER THIRTY

<hr>

The Long Way Home

Peter lay on the table in his family's kitchen, his breathing coming in short gasps. His mother, Mrs. Sullivan, held his hand and wept silent tears.

Nessa pressed a wet cloth to his forehead, then stepped away. She felt sick with the horrible truth: Peter was dying.

And it was her fault.

The room was busy with friends of his parents. They whispered stories about snakebites and remedies, how this person survived, this one didn't. Frantic efforts were made with poultices and lancing the wound. The surgeon rushed over from the hospital, but after putting a stethoscope to Peter's chest and listening for some moments, he shook his head.

There was nothing anyone could do.

Nessa looked through the open door to the prairie. What had seemed beautiful and safe an hour ago now seemed like a nightmare. Her heart twisted inside her. She was tormented by the thought that if she'd been more attentive she could have kept Peter from wandering off. How could she have been so distracted?

And the way people were looking at her — Nessa could see it in their eyes. They were blaming her.

"Careless girl," one of them had said to the back of her head.

"Unfit to be a teacher," said another.

Please, God, Nessa prayed, *let Peter live. . . . Save him. . . . He's only six. . . . Please forgive me for not watching him more carefully. . . .*

A mournful wail pierced the air. Nessa turned to see Peter's mother cradling him on her lap.

"No . . . no . . ." she was crying.

Peter's arm flopped to the side. His face had turned pale blue and his lips were white. His father the lieutenant lifted the wounded hand and lay it across his son's chest, tenderly embracing his wife.

Nessa couldn't bear the sight. She rushed outside, not thinking, not knowing where she was going. How could a day of celebration turn so ugly?

More people were gathered on the porch, and they turned to watch her. Nessa started to run.

Why, God. Why . . . why? she cried to herself. *It's not fair. Why take Peter and not the Cooley Boys, who murdered the teacher?*

At the creek, she dropped to her knees and wept. She didn't notice the water lapping at her skirt, getting her wet.

If only I'd prayed more. . . . If only . . . Her list was long, full of things she could have, should have done. *Where were you, God? Why didn't you warn me about the snake?*

Nessa was in anguish imagining Peter's curiosity and

how he probably was trying to protect a baby rabbit. What did he think when the rattler launched itself at his hand — was he afraid — did he suffer? When he called but no one came, did he think they didn't care? At this, she sobbed. She tore the ribbons from her hair and with her fingers clawed out her braids.

It had been a terrible mistake to come to Prairie River and even worse to think she could care for children. They were right. She wasn't fit to be a teacher. *Why did you let me come here, Lord? Why didn't you stop me? Peter might still be alive if I had married the preacher and stayed . . .*

Nessa woke to the soothing sound of the stream washing over rocks. She brushed the sand from her cheek, then rolled on her back to look up at the willows. Dappled sunlight cast lacy shadows over the riverbank. Though the air was hot, it felt cool lying on the wet sand. She closed her eyes, listening to the noisy clicks of cicadas coming from the prairie and wished she could sleep forever. The thought of returning to town renewed her grief.

Finally, she rinsed her hands in the cold water, then splashed her face. While she was wringing out the hem of her dress, she noticed someone across the creek, watching her.

Rolly. He was barefoot, sitting with his arms wrapped around his knees.

At the sight of her friend, she began crying again.

"It ain't your fault, Nessa, it just ain't." He rolled up his cuffs and waded over.

He took her hand to help her up. "Come on. . . . Ma's worried about you and so's Mr. Button. Besides, I've been waitin' two hours for you to wake up."

They walked the long way home, stopping by the school-house. Nessa went to Peter's desk and ran her hand over its smooth wood. She looked underneath at the narrow shelf where he had stowed his lessons. His pencil was there with a poem he had written in large block letters, on the blank side of a newspaper.

MY CAT HAS LEGS
MY DOG IS GREEN
MY MA COOKS EGGS
WITH PORK AND BEANS.

Nessa smiled. She knew Peter's dog wasn't green, but she liked how he put the words together, anyway. She folded the paper into her sleeve, to take to his mother. That is, if Mrs. Sullivan was willing to see her.

They walked to the garden by crossing another creek. Four buckets of water were still there in the hot sun, one tipped over. Nessa wanted to run away, never to set foot here again because this was where they'd last seen Peter playing. But she knew the garden would die if no one tended it.

Rolly began dribbling water along a row of flowers, then Nessa did the same. For the next hour, they filled the buckets in the stream and carried them sloshing to the garden.

When they stopped to rest, they looked out over the golden prairie. Thunderheads were rising over the horizon, with fingers of sunlight streaming downward. The wind swished the grass about their knees and blew Nessa's unbraided hair.

"Reckon Peter's up there with the angels?" asked Rolly.

"I reckon so."

"Jesus said children have angels watching over them, and these angels see the face of God, that's what my pa read to me from the Bible. But I don't get why the angels didn't protect Peter from the snake." Rolly reached for a sunflower that stood his height and began plucking the yellow petals, tossing them to the wind.

Exhausted from crying, Nessa let out a shuddering sigh. "I don't know, either," she said. "What if . . . Maybe the angels *were* there. Then they helped us find him so he wouldn't die all alone. Maybe it was just Peter's time; God was calling him home. It doesn't make sense to me, it isn't at all fair, but God has His own reasons."

Nessa couldn't tell him she was thinking of leaving Prairie River. The thought of Peter's parents and the sorrow she'd seen in their eyes now brought more tears. Would they ever forgive her? She wasn't sure she could ever face them or anyone else in town.

Rolly patted her shoulder, trying to comfort her. "Ma also said Peter's in heaven where there ain't no more crying or things to hurt you. Even the lion and the lamb will be friends. I like that, knowing Peter's safe."

"Me, too," said Nessa, but anguish still filled her heart.

As they walked toward town, she noticed the path to the garden had green sprouts along each side. A bittersweet smile came to Nessa's face. All the water Peter spilled from his pail, all the trips back and forth from the creek, had caused something to start growing.

CHAPTER THIRTY-ONE

———≫◆≪———

"Who Makes the Woeful Heart to Sing"

The funeral was the next morning. Due to the summer heat, the body needed to be buried quickly. The cemetery was outside town, a small arrangement of wooden crosses and markers, as Prairie River was a young settlement. Four fresh graves were for soldiers who had died of cholera a week earlier.

Nessa felt faint from the sun. In the distance, she could see a stagecoach leaving the fort, its six horses running with the wind. How she wished she were on it, headed back to Missouri, but she couldn't leave without saying good-bye to Peter.

After the minister's prayer, Mrs. Applewood nudged Nessa. She whispered so close to Nessa's ear, it sounded like a hiss. "We knew an orphan like you would end up doing something we would all regret."

"Madam," said Nessa, her voice breaking, "that is one of the cruelest things anyone has ever said to me."

This time she didn't hide her tears. As the small wooden coffin was lowered into the ground, Nessa wept with a broken heart. She had loved Peter. When her eyes went to his mother, she realized the grieving woman had been looking at her.

Peter's auntie began singing. Her voice was beautiful. Fanny Jo and Laura joined in, then the others. Nessa loved this hymn, but such was her sorrow she could only whisper the words.

Fairest Lord Jesus,
Ruler of all nature,
O thou of God and man the Son;
Thee will I cherish,
Thee will I honor,
Thou, my soul's glory, joy, and crown . . .

Fair are the meadows,
Fairer still the woodlands,
Robed in the blooming garb of spring;
Jesus is fairer,
Jesus is purer,
Who makes the woeful heart to sing.

It's so unfair, thought Nessa. With all her heart she wanted to honor Jesus by singing, but she felt numb. There was too much she didn't understand. Later, when she returned to the cemetery alone, she read the grave markers. She was further distressed to learn that most were for children and babies who hadn't lived more than a few months.

This made her think about Mrs. Bell's son, who was about six weeks old. What if he fell sick and died like all these here? *"Oh, Jesus,"* she prayed aloud, *"please protect little Oliver. . . . Let him live and grow up to be a man who honors You. . . . Please protect all the children. . . . Lord, please help me understand."*

Nessa knelt in the tall grass where no one could see her. Gazing up at the pale blue sky, she pleaded with God to comfort Peter's family and to mend the ache in her own heart. *Where are You, Jesus? Miss Eva says You're alive and that You are close to those who grieve. . . . I want to hear Your voice.* She strained to listen, but heard only the wind swirl through the golden stalks.

As she walked back to town, an idea came to her.

With Rolly's help, she dug up a tiny oak tree from the bottomland, about three feet tall. They wrapped its roots in wet rags, set it carefully in his wagon, then rounded up the other children. Big Howard sat in back with a shovel, a hammer and nails, and scraps of lumber from behind the carpenter's shop. Minnie, Augusta, and Lucy each put a pail of water into the wagon, Ivy walked alongside, carrying an armful of sunflowers.

By sunset, they had planted the sapling near Peter's grave, watered it, and built a small fence around it to protect its thin trunk from animals. With rope, they secured it to the fence so it wouldn't bend in the wind. Then they placed a flower on the marker of each child and infant, fifteen in all.

Nessa knew this would have pleased Peter.

The next afternoon, Nessa walked to the sutler's compound, where a seamstress had a tiny shop. She avoided

Officers' Row in case Peter's mother might see her. Nessa desperately wanted to say she was sorry, but didn't think she could do so right now without falling apart. She didn't want to make Mrs. Sullivan feel worse.

Keeping her head down, Nessa hurried on her errand. She wanted to surprise Mrs. Lockett with some lace for an apron she was sewing. When she stepped inside, two ladies were there with baskets over their arms, deep in conversation.

". . . and she's not saying?" one of them asked.

"It's obvious," said the other.

Then the seamstress leaned over the counter to whisper to her friends. Ignoring Nessa, she said, "Their father was a senator, you know — if he ever finds out . . ."

Soon enough, Nessa knew they were discussing Fanny Jo. She was filled with curiosity and tempted to ask for further details. Instead, she just nodded in greeting. She didn't want to betray the sisters' secret, although she didn't know precisely what that secret was.

"Good day," she said while handing the seamstress twenty cents. She recognized the ladies from church. They each had children too young for school, and one of them was expecting a baby. This she could tell by the smock that hung over the woman's full middle.

"Hello, Nessa," they said in unison. They fell silent, staring at her until she opened the door. Just as Nessa stepped outside, they started talking again. Her face felt hot with embarrassment when she heard her name again and realized they were now discussing her.

"She's not going to teach *my* little boy," one of the women said.

". . . should be run out of town," said another.

Nessa rushed home, gave Mrs. Lockett the lace, and not until she had run upstairs and buried her face in her buffalo robe, did she let herself cry. At least Mrs. Applewood had said those awful things to her face.

CHAPTER THIRTY-TWO

The Gift

For three weeks Nessa stayed home, the Lockett family her quiet companions. At times, her devastation over Peter's death was unbearable, and knowing that people blamed her increased her anguish. She ventured outside only to fetch water, rake the barn, and hang laundry on the line. The sweltering heat made her feel listless.

By the end of July, Nessa had been in Prairie River for three months. One day, Big Howard came to visit with a picnic basket. He set it on the porch, then knocked.

"Surprise!" he said, when Nessa opened the door. She was barefoot because she'd been mopping the floors. Noticing the basket and that it was jiggling, she smiled at him.

"Hello, Howard. What d'you have there?"

"Guess."

"A rabbit?"

"Better!"

"Kittens?"

"Even better!"

To Nessa, the only thing better would be a horse, but still she was excited to know what was inside. She kneeled to peek under the lid. Four wiggly puppies looked up at her. They were pale yellow.

"Oh!" she cried, scooping two of them into her arms. "Where'd you find them?"

"They're Peter's. His ma brought them to our house. There's a note here for you." He gave her a cream-colored envelope that had lace along the flap. There was a light fragrance of perfume.

As Nessa held the letter, her hands began shaking. She had not seen Peter's mother since the funeral. Would there be harsh words? . . . A scolding? She set the puppies in her lap and took a deep breath. Carefully, she pulled out a crisp sheet of stationery and unfolded it.

Dear Nessa,
Peter said that you loved living things as much as he did and that you were his favorite teacher. Please accept one of Yellow Dog's puppies for your own. It would have made him very happy.

  Lieutenant Sullivan and I know you would never have done anything to harm our son. Thank you for saving his poem. Your kind Mrs. Lockett brought it over to us.
Yours Sincerely,
Mrs. Sullivan

Nessa tried to speak, but felt a catch in her throat. She hugged the puppies, not caring that Howard could see she was crying. *Thank you, Lord, that they don't blame me.* Nessa felt the rapid heartbeats against her cheek. She smelled the fur and at once recognized that familiar, pleasant scent she had noticed in her buffalo robe. Did she have a dog long ago, before being sent to the orphanage? How she wished she could remember.

"Howard," she said, "would you please take the puppies until Mrs. Lockett gives me permission to keep one? Thank you so much. I know you'll take good care of them."

At supper, the table was crowded with five new guests, travelers on their way to New Mexico Territory. One was a Catholic priest who would be living in the pueblo of Santa Fe.

Throughout the meal, Nessa tried to make polite conversation but all she could think of was the puppy and what she'd say to Mrs. Lockett once the dishes were done. Her interest perked up, however, when the priest said he had met a minister in Independence who wanted to come preach in Prairie River.

Nessa held her breath for a moment. "Do you know his name?" she asked.

He looked at the ceiling and squinted, trying to remember.

"Uh, no," said the priest, "I don't remember that much about him. He was about my height, a pleasant fellow, though not given to much humor. During our conversation, the gentleman spoke so slowly it seemed he was about to fall asleep."

Nessa's mouth went dry. Slowly, she touched her head. "Did he have hair?"

"Like me." He laughed, removing his skullcap. He was bald on top. "Why? Do you know him, miss?"

His question hung in the air. She felt sick with dread. Maybe there were two ministers fitting the same description. "I may know *of* him," she said.

After the pots were put away and she wiped the table, Nessa took the wet towels outside to hang on the line. The air was hot enough that things would dry overnight. Minnie helped her carry water to the henhouse, then gather eggs for tomorrow's breakfast. They set them in a basket by the back door before fetching water for Mrs. Lockett's vegetable garden.

"Why did you almost cry, Nessa?" she asked. "I seen you were upset. . . . You know, when Ma was dishing up the cobbler . . . when the priest was talking. . . ."

They were at the creek fetching water. Nessa set her bucket on the grassy path to look at Minnie. She was touched that this little one had noticed her discomfort at supper.

"Know what?" she said, giving the girl's pigtail a playful tug. "If I could pick anyone in the world to be my little sister, I'd pick you."

"Really?"

"See yonder, how pretty that is?" Nessa pointed across the prairie to the setting sun that had just touched the horizon. In seconds, it slipped out of sight, leaving a burst of pink and violet to paint the sky. "Minnie," she said, "the most beautiful sunset on earth isn't half as special as you are."

Nessa sat in bed, the candle on her nightstand casting long shadows against the walls. She was distraught thinking Reverend McDuff might come to Prairie River and wondered if he actually knew she was here or if it was just coincidence. She also wondered if she should confide in someone. Albert would understand and so would Miss Eva, but they were so far away.

A dreadful thought occurred to her. What would people think if they learned she'd run away from her wedding, on top of Peter's death? No one would ever trust her.

Her Bible was open in her lap. Often she felt peaceful when reading Scripture, but tonight she didn't know where to look. Flipping through pages, her eyes fell on a passage in the eleventh book of Matthew.

Come unto me, all ye that labour and are heavy laden and I will give you rest. Take my yoke upon you, and learn of me; for I am meek and lowly in heart: and ye shall find rest unto your souls. For my yoke is easy and my burden is light.

She closed her eyes, sighing deeply. *Jesus, I reckon that's me, heavy laden about what happened to Peter. I'm sad about his mother and father and sad how his sister, Poppy, won't have her big brother to grow up with. And while I'm here talking to You, Lord, I am tired — so tired — of worrying about the preacher coming after me. Jesus, if You really are here, please help me with these burdens and . . .*

There was a gentle knock on the door.

"Yes?"

Mrs. Lockett peeked in. Her hair lay in a thick braid over her shoulder. She wore a nightgown made from white cotton, embroidered around the neck with blue flowers. "Forgive me, dear, if I'm intruding. . . ."

"No, it's all right. Come in, please."

She sat on the end of the bed and looked at Nessa with concern in her eyes. "You didn't seem your usual self tonight. I ain't meanin' to pry, but if there's anything you want to talk about, anything atall, we can . . ."

"Oh, Mrs. Lockett, there is. Did you see the puppies Howard brought over?"

She smiled at Nessa. "Would you like one?"

"Oh, yes! Please."

"Then we best have Rolly make a collar. For its bed you can use that old blanket — we washed it last Monday, remember? The gray one with red trim."

Nessa threw her arms around the woman's neck. "Thank you . . . thank you."

Mrs. Lockett flushed and leaned back to cup Nessa's cheeks in her hands. "Well, my dear, if I had any notion that such a small thing could make you so happy . . . my, my . . ." A moment passed, then she stood up. "Well, I reckon I'll see you in the morning, honey. Sleep well."

Nessa stared at the door after she left, her heart still burning inside her. There *was* more she needed to say. Suddenly, she found herself hurrying down the hall.

"Mrs. Lockett . . ."

CHAPTER THIRTY-THREE

The Officer's Wife

Mrs. Lockett's room was over the kitchen. A patchwork quilt covered a bed with two feather pillows at its head. The oil lamp on her dresser was small, just four inches high, and it cast a soft glow. Her window looked out toward the trail. Since everyone else had gone to bed, it was quiet throughout the house with just a sighing of the wind in the eaves. Motioning for Nessa to sit on a stool, Mrs. Lockett glanced out over the dark prairie, then turned to her.

"I'm listenin', honey."

Nessa was surprised she was able to relate her story without crying. It was as if she was talking about someone else when she told about the orphanage, about Mr. Carey and Reverend McDuff. She described the wonderful Miss Eva and the other children.

"I didn't want to leave those darling little ones or Miss Eva," she said. "But I was afraid of Mr. Carey. He had a terrible temper and sometimes used a whip. He said the only thing I was good for was to be a servant or to be the wife of Reverend McDuff. The minister wasn't a bad man, but he was dreary and sad and pale. His sermons made me feel that there wasn't much beauty or hope in life. How could I marry someone who didn't believe in happiness?"

"You're a smart girl, dear. Go on."

"Every time someone mentions a minister coming to Prairie River I panic, worrying it might be Reverend McDuff coming to claim me. And Mr. Carey is probably so mad and humiliated that I ran away, I wouldn't be surprised if he comes after me, too.

"Oh, Mrs. Lockett, most of all I miss Albert." Nessa's voice wavered; her eyes filled with tears. "It was so nice to have a true friend. We kept each other's secrets and could talk about anything. Since we're both orphans and grew up in the same house, there's a lot we understand about each other without having to say words. I think I made a terrible mistake coming here. . . . Peter would still be alive . . . if only . . ." She was unable to continue.

She covered her face with her hands and wept. Mrs. Lockett reached for Nessa and wrapped her arms around her. "There, there, my dear, it's all right."

The clock downstairs chimed ten. A gust of wind rattled the windowpane.

Finally, Nessa looked up. "I am very, very sorry for all the trouble I've caused — so many people hate me, and I don't know what to do or how to tell everyone I'm sorry — I thought God was saying I should leave Missouri, I really did. Then I thought He was leading me to be the schoolteacher, but now everything's so mixed up. Maybe Peter's death is a sign I'm supposed to go back . . . that I was never supposed to come."

"Look at me, Nessa."

Nessa lifted her head.

Mrs. Lockett took her Bible from the table by her bed and opened it. "These pages are worn thin by all my years of searchin' and readin' and pleadin' with God. What you didn't know, honey, is that for months and months I've been prayin' for my husband to return — he's a captain, been gone almost three years. He filled our house with joy, he did. Always cheerful, so ready with a kind word and generous to strangers. A leader. In fact, last letter said he'd met President Lincoln on horseback, right outside the White House. But since the war ended, we haven't heard from him. Rolly stopped his jokin' and never talked, and Minnie refused to go to school, cried herself to sleep every night. Lord knows my own heart was breakin'. The reason we're not living on Officers' Row is because that good man ain't here."

The oil lamp began to sputter, so Mrs. Lockett leaned over to turn up the wick. Light glowed in the corner. Her face appeared tired, but her eyes were bright. She looked at Nessa with tenderness.

"My dear, what I'm trying to tell you is when you knocked on our door that day and were so wet and cold and fallin' asleep on your feet, I knew a ray of sunshine had come into our lives. I just knew it. Your sweet spirit touched my heart and more than anything I wanted you to be a part of our family. My children adore you, Nessa. You see, God answered *my* prayers by bringin' you to Prairie River. He's a God of love and miracles and wonderful surprises, so I'm still askin' Him to bring my

Charlie home. And askin' Him to keep you with us. You have so much to offer our family and this town."

Mrs. Lockett placed her hand against Nessa's cheek. Her skin was rough but had the good smell of lavender soap. "Honey, whilst I've only known you a few months, I can see you are solid as gold. If you truly believed leaving Missouri was the right thing to do, then I believe it, too. But no matter which path we take, Nessa, there will always be trying times. You can count on it. Faith is believing that God has a plan for our lives even when things seem to be falling apart. Trust Him with all your heart, dear. Trust yourself. Your faith is bigger than you realize."

Nessa clutched the woman's rough hand. "Oh, Mrs. Lockett, I love you." Nessa felt overwhelmed with happiness for she couldn't remember ever having said those three words.

The next morning, Nessa walked to Mr. Filmore's store to see if the stage had arrived with mail for her. Then she went to the newspaper office to show Mr. Button her puppy. She held it in her arms so it wouldn't run loose and knock over the pail of ink.

"That's a fine animal you got there." He stroked the soft fur with the back of his hand because his fingers were smudged with ink. "Looks like some kind of water dog the way its ears hang down. . . . Say, did you see the news today? Word came in on last night's stage . . . Here . . ." He reached for the paper he'd just rolled off the press and waved it so the ink would dry.

"It happened some days ago," he said. "In Washington, D.C., they finally hung those criminals involved in Lincoln's assassination. . . . Seems that one of 'em was Mrs. Mary Surratt, a woman with three children. . . . They tied her dress around her knees so it wouldn't fly up when she plunged through the trapdoor. . . . Awful, the whole thing's just awful."

Nessa held her puppy closer to her chest. "You mean they killed a mother? They really hung her?"

"Yes, ma'am," he answered. "And it's my recollection that Mrs. Surratt is the first lady executed by our government. . . . By the way, you should know the Cooley Boys robbed a stage last week and they're stirring up trouble along the trail, but we've got soldiers here watching out for us. Just you stay close to the fort now."

While Nessa considered this, he broke off a piece of sandwich he'd been eating and gave it to the puppy, patting its head. Mr. Button's eyes crinkled at the edges when he smiled. Nessa loved it when he talked on and on about the news.

"Say, not to change the subject, but d'you know what you're going to call your new friend here?" He fed it a bite of crust that had dropped onto his large stomach.

"Not yet." But then, thinking of Peter's poem, she said, "Oh, yes! Green. That's her name." Nessa blinked fast. She ached remembering he was gone.

Seeing her tears, Mr. Button reached in his vest pocket for his handkerchief and offered it to her. It was wrinkled and stuck together in parts.

"I apologize. It's the only clean one I have," he said.

"I'm all right, thank you, Mr. Button." She looked at the bushy curls of his mustache and the stains on his shirt. Her heart melted with affection for him. He was the second person in two days who had made her feel like a much-loved daughter.

Nessa was relieved to know that not everyone in town was against her.

CHAPTER THIRTY-FOUR

———◆———

A Late Night Arrival

The next afternoon, clouds lay heavy over the prairie. Heat made the air feel like an oven. Thunder rumbled in the distance. Nessa walked with Minnie to the cemetery, each carrying a pail of water. A hot wind blew their skirts against their legs and wisps of hair around their faces. Green loped alongside, often stopping to sniff a flower or pounce on an insect. She was two months old, pudgy as a bear cub, and already responding to Nessa's whistle.

As they approached the knoll near Peter's grave, they saw Big Howard standing by the little oak tree, tightening the rope that helped it stand straight. An empty bucket was at his side.

"Hullo, Teacher." Pointing to the top of the tree he said, "It's growin' fast, see?" It stood nearly as tall as his shoulder and its leaves were rustling in the wind as if it were already a big tree.

"It surely is, Howard . . . thanks to all your watering." Then noticing a frown on his face, she asked, "Everything all right?"

He stared at the ground by her feet. "Miss Nessa, my

aunt wants to know when you're leaving Prairie River. She and Uncle say you're unfit to be a teacher and besides, you wore out your welcome."

Nessa looked toward town, not wanting him to see how his question upset her. Two new houses were being built from sod strips and lumber hauled in this week from woodlands farther east. Even from here, they could hear hammering and the hum of saws. She liked it that new folks were moving in. New folks meant the possibility of new friends.

She felt a raindrop on her arm and watched the wet circle spread through the cloth of her sleeve, then another fell and another. Looking up at the darkening sky she said, "Howard, what do you think about this, what your aunt and uncle believe?"

"Dunno."

"Well, I would suggest you think hard about your own opinion before passing along someone else's. By the way, do I know your aunt and uncle?"

"You seen 'em," he said. "They're sutlers . . . the Applewoods."

Oh, thought Nessa, *now some things make sense.* She kept her angry opinion to herself. In a voice that was calmer than she felt, she asked, "Howard, why are they so . . . prickly?" It was the kindest word she could think of at that moment.

Rain was beginning to pelt them, spotting the dirt. Howard grabbed his pail and Nessa's and began hurrying along the path toward the fort.

"Well . . ." he began. He raised his voice to be heard

above the hissing of rain. "I reckon they're mad cuz Yanks burned down their plantation last year. They lost everything and all their slaves escaped. Me and Pa and Ma were already here in Prairie River so they came, too. Kin in Mississippi gave 'em a wagon of provisions to help 'em start over. . . ."

Nessa had never heard Big Howard say so much, and now she didn't know how to respond. She picked up Green to carry in her arms because the puppy was having trouble keeping up with their brisk pace. Minnie clutched Nessa's skirt, running alongside in the rain. The memory of little Mary doing the same thing in the orphanage made Nessa smile, but her thoughts quickly returned to the Applewoods. *Lots of folks have tragedies,* she thought, *but don't turn hateful like they have.*

Why should she keep trying to be nice to them?

But she remembered something Miss Eva often told her: *People who are sour are those who most need love.*

Nessa just didn't feel like loving Mr. and Mrs. Applewood.

When Nessa woke the next morning, Fanny Jo was leaning over her, whispering her name. She opened her eyes. It was not yet dawn. Through the open curtains, she saw the sky was bluish pink, perhaps an hour before sunrise. She ran her hand along the fur of her buffalo robe until she felt her puppy. Green was asleep between her and the wall, with her four paws in the air.

"What's wrong?" Nessa asked. She was tired and didn't want to get up.

"Hurry," said Fanny Jo. "Mrs. Lockett said I could wake you. Get dressed; there's a surprise down at the sutler's."

Nessa bolted up. "Did the stage . . . ?"

"Yes, it came in late last night, after midnight — hurry!"

CHAPTER THIRTY-FIVE

The White Rose

A small crowd gathered at Mr. Filmore's store. Mr. Button greeted Nessa when she walked in by taking Green from her arms and handing her a long brass key.

"This came with it, my dear."

Next to the potbellied stove, which was not lit this hot August morning, sat a trunk two feet tall. It was made of tin, painted green and red with oak ribs in between. Silver adorned the rounded corners and a silver lock secured its lid. A tag pasted on top read:

> NESSA CLEMENS, 15 APRIL 1851
> DELIVER TO PRAIRIE RIVER, KANSAS
> POSTAGE PAID

Nessa had never seen anything so intriguing. It had her name and birth date, but was it really hers?

Fanny Jo said, "Isn't it something? Laura and I were here last night to pick up mail and there it was. Mr. Button said to let you sleep, but by five A.M., we couldn't wait any longer. . . . It feels like Christmas."

Laura clapped her hands with excitement. "Oh, do open it, won't you, Nessa?"

Nessa didn't know how to explain what this trunk meant to her.

It might have nothing important inside, but then it might have everything, whatever that meant. If Miss Eva had known its contents, she didn't say so in her letter.

Mr. Button noticed Nessa's uncertainty. "Pardon us all for staring," he said, "it's just that Prairie River rarely gets mail bigger than a letter and certainly nothing so colorful."

When she looked up at him, her eyes were moist. "Uh . . ." She hesitated. "I think I'd like to open it in my room, if someone can oblige —"

Before she finished her sentence, Rolly and Mr. Button each grabbed a leather handle and carried it out the door. Along Pawnee Creek they shuffled, stopping twice to adjust their hands for the trunk was heavy. Green trotted beside Nessa to the path where the small procession then headed for the boardinghouse. They hauled it up the porch steps, through the parlor, and past the kitchen — where Mrs. Lockett was serving hotcakes to her guests — then upstairs to Nessa's room, which was at the end of the hallway.

They lowered her trunk to the floor and slid it under the window that looked out upon the prairie. There was just enough space for her to sit on her bed with her knees touching the silver latch.

Nessa regarded those who now gathered. Fanny Jo and Laura stood in the doorway behind Mr. Button. Minnie was there with Rolly. He dusted off his hands, then leaned down to pick up the puppy. No one said a word.

From downstairs came the familiar noise of an iron skillet being moved over the stovetop and voices from the guests. There was a good smell of coffee. Nessa loved her new home and the friends who were watching her. But she was torn. She wanted privacy yet she didn't want to be alone.

"I don't know what to do," she finally confessed to them.

Fanny Jo said, "Would you like us to leave, dear?"

Tears stung Nessa's eyes. "I don't know . . . I . . ." She was afraid, but of what she wasn't sure, and she was embarrassed to be crying in front of everyone. What would they think if they knew she wanted to return to Missouri? Wiping her cheeks with her sleeve, she drew in a deep breath, then took the key from her clutched fingers.

It fit into the lock, clicking when she turned it.

She ran her hands over the lid, feeling the cool tin and admiring its colors: The red resembled brick and the green was like a pale olive. The silver corners shone.

Nessa lifted the lid.

A scent released from the past greeted her and without realizing why, a sob caught in her throat. Something was so familiar, but what was it?

A quilt lay folded on top. It was made from squares of cloth patched together, various patterns of yellow and white. She buried her face in it and wept, gathering the soft material in her fingers.

Now she remembered.

This was from her mother's dress. Somewhere long

ago, Nessa had laid her cheek on her lap. The colors and texture — cotton worn smooth — and the scent of soap and rosemary were the same.

How old was she when she last touched that dress . . . three, four?

She felt her puppy pawing at her knee, trying to jump onto the bed. When she looked up, she realized everyone had left the room.

Part of Nessa wanted to dig through the contents and immediately see everything. Part of her wanted to go slowly, discover one layer at a time, to think and try to remember. Her heart ached with something she didn't understand. She sat on her bed, facing the trunk and the window above it. The sun was now an hour high, rising into a low bank of clouds. A warm breeze pressed against the curtains. The air smelled of rain. Nessa didn't know where to begin.

Mrs. Lockett called Nessa to lunch. When she didn't appear at the table, she climbed the stairs to see if she was all right.

Nessa's door was still open. On her bed were packets of letters tied with blue ribbon, some books and folded clothing, household items.

"I've taken everything out — twice — and am putting it back again," she told Mrs. Lockett, holding up a small box. "I'm not sure what any of it means. There's just so much — do you think it's all right if I go through it bit by bit?"

Mrs. Lockett kissed the top of her head, then sat on the bed. "Yes, dear, I do. It's your very own treasure chest for you to do with as you see fit."

Nessa lifted a large book. It was heavy and covered with a red flannel shirt, its sleeves knotted around it for protection. Mrs. Lockett helped untie the cloth and carefully unwrap it.

It was several inches thick, bound in leather with HOLY BIBLE stamped on the front cover. Engraved in the bottom right-hand corner was a name: H. L. CLEMENS.

Nessa ran her finger over the gold lettering. "I wonder who this is," she whispered.

CHAPTER THIRTY-SIX

<hr/>

Unwelcome Visitors

During the next few days, Nessa studied the front pages of the Bible, trying to memorize her family tree. It was a joyous discovery to learn her middle name was Ann. *Vanessa Ann Clemens.* She said it again and again, until it felt a part of her. She also learned that she was born AT SUNRISE, ON A COLD, SPRING MORNING, 1851, IN RACINE, WISCONSIN, according to a penciled note in the margin.

She tried to piece together the story of her parents. Her mother, Claire Christine Nielsen, was from Denmark. When she saw her father's name — Howard Lewis Clemens — she caught her breath. This was his Bible, his handwriting, his brief note: WIFE, CLAIRE CHRISTINE, TODAY DIED OF CHILDBED FEVER IN RACINE, BUT THE TWINS LIVE.

Nessa was sitting on her bed when she read this. *Twins?* Leaning back against the wall, she closed her eyes. Her father's note stirred a vague memory — a house filled with people and a neighbor holding two tiny infants. Her father stood quietly by a bed as someone pulled a sheet up over her mother's gray face. . . .

Nessa's eyes flew open. She stood up to look out the window. The morning was fresh with an immense blue sky; birds were singing. The world was alive with beauty. She didn't want to think about death. It grieved her to think what her father must have felt that day when he took pen in hand and opened his Bible.

Lord, please help me remember something else. . . . Something good . . .

She washed her hands and face in the basin, then hurried downstairs to help cook breakfast.

After Minnie and Nessa dried the dishes and put them away, they hung their aprons on hooks and put on their sunbonnets.

"We're going to visit Mrs. Bell," said Nessa, tying the ribbon under Minnie's chin. "Green is coming, too, aren't you, girl?" Nessa bent down to pet the puppy's yellow head as her wagging tail swished the floor. She felt happy Mrs. Bell had invited them for lunch. It was to be her first stepping out since Peter died.

It was hot, even walking along the bottomland. They followed the river to above where the buffalo had been, where the grass wasn't trampled and soiled. When they stopped to eat wild plums and drink, they took off their shoes to wade. Looking around to make sure no one was nearby, Nessa convinced Minnie they should strip down to their camisoles and jump in.

"Come on!" Nessa cried as she plowed into the cold

water. Her puppy was right behind her, paddling with its nose in the air. The current pulled them into a shallow pool where the girls dunked their heads and came up laughing, gasping for breath. As Nessa grabbed Minnie's hands to twirl her around, she noticed a flash of color — blue — downstream, around the bend.

She put her finger to her lips, signaling Minnie to be quiet, then pulled Green's collar so she would swim toward her.

Indians. At least a dozen, watering their horses. Some of the men wore only breechcloths. Others wore blue army jackets and the hats of soldiers. Some had long black hair hanging over their shoulders; others wore braids.

A cold fear made Nessa's heart start racing. She led Minnie back to shore where they hid themselves behind the drooping branches of a willow. The puppy shook off her dripping fur. Nessa nearly panicked in her hurry to dress when she realized how hard it was to pull clothes on over wet skin. All the while, she watched the men through the branches. They were laughing among themselves and speaking in a language she'd never heard before. Without bothering to fasten every button, she and Minnie crept upstream along the riverbank, carrying their shoes. She hoped the water would hide any noise from their steps and she prayed Green wouldn't bark.

After several minutes, the schoolhouse came into sight. Nessa looked behind them and, seeing no one, grabbed Minnie's hand and raced ahead.

Once inside she said, "Hurry, Minnie, help me," and

began pushing desks in front of the door. She knew the men could break windows if they wanted to get in, but this made her feel better. The puppy jumped on Nessa, thinking they were playing a game.

Minnie's pigtails dripped onto her shoulders and sleeves. As Nessa helped lace up her shoes, she started praying aloud. There wasn't time for folded hands and closed eyes.

"Jesus," she began, but her mind went blank. All she could think about was how afraid she was and how Minnie was depending on her. "Jesus . . ." she started again. Still no words came. She touched Minnie's cheek to reassure the girl, then crawled to the window.

Slowly, she pulled herself up.

Indians were riding toward the schoolhouse.

With a sick feeling, Nessa slumped against the wall.

"Minnie, can you be brave?"

Minnie nodded, but her lip quivered.

"Good," said Nessa, "because that is what we must be right now. Those Indians are coming. I have an idea, come."

Together, they pushed the desks back in place, then hurried to the front of the classroom. Though Nessa's insides were shaking, she began writing sums on the blackboard. If the warriors came inside, she wanted them to see a teacher working calmly with her student, not hiding behind a barricade of desks. She would not let them see the terror she felt.

The sounds of hoofbeats thundered outside the window. She could see riders pass by, then a moment later, pass the other window going in the opposite direction.

They were circling the schoolhouse.

Nessa managed to say, "Keep your eyes on me, Minnie. Let's subtract twelve from twenty-four. . . ." While writing numbers with the chalk, she silently counted as the horsemen circled. *Three, now four times . . .* The windows rattled with vibrations from the hooves; dust rose up. It seemed their circle was growing closer. Nessa started a silent prayer.

Lord, I don't know what to do if they come in. . . . Please help us. . . . I don't want to die or for Mrs. Lockett to lose her daughter, not after she has had so much faith in me. . . . Nessa felt like crying, but didn't want to frighten Minnie any further. The little girl was trembling at her side.

At last, the noise stopped. *They're getting off their horses and coming in.* She held her breath, waiting for the door to swing open, afraid to look.

A full minute passed.

Finally, she turned toward the window. They were riding away. As she watched their trail of dust, she lowered herself to her chair. Her mouth was too dry to swallow. She held her hand over her heart as if doing so could slow its wild beating. Green was leaning against Nessa's leg as if to comfort her.

Minnie burst into tears. "I hate Indians. . . . I hate them!"

Nessa pulled her close. Their sleeves were still wet from their dripping hair. "Hush, now. They're gone. They didn't hurt us, see? They were just curious, and we don't need to hate them for that."

Minnie continued to wail.

"God loves them the same as He loves you and me," Nessa said. "He made all of us in His image. . . ."

"I don't care! He made rattlesnakes, too. . . ." She buried her face in Nessa's dress, sobbing Peter's name, now grieving for him.

Nessa's faith in God was just words in her head right now. She felt weak with anxiety, wondering why it was easy to feel peaceful when there was no danger, no snakes, no Indians, no reminder of Reverend McDuff. No townsfolk to criticize her.

Her forehead felt tight with tears that she wouldn't allow herself to cry. There was so much she wanted to understand, but at this moment she knew only one thing.

"Minnie," she said, looking at her wet face, "they didn't hurt us. We're all right. Now let's go home."

Later that evening, after everyone in the house had turned in, Nessa couldn't sleep. She crept downstairs, followed by her puppy, to sit in the yard where it was cooler. From a garden bench, she drank in the dark beauty of the night. Stars, so many millions, more than she could ever count, were shimmering with tiny wiggles of light.

God, You know exactly how many there are and You call each star by name. . . . How do You do that and watch over us, too? Thank You for protecting Minnie and me today. . . . Thank You for giving me courage. . . .

She felt weak remembering her encounter that afternoon, how on the walk home she vomited in the brush.

Of course, Minnie had shouted the news as soon as they ran up the back porch. The news traveled fast. Soldiers were alerted. Mr. Button was soon standing in the kitchen with other townsfolk, writing in his notepad.

"You're a brave one, you are," they told Nessa.

One of the woodcutters hired by the army was not as supportive. "My boy'll be big enough to go to school next year, but it ain't safe havin' a schoolhouse so far from the fort with only a young thing like you watchin' over 'em."

"They were just curious," Nessa said again. "They didn't do any harm."

Rolly crossed his arms like the men in the room and said, "Those Indians better never hurt you, that's all I can say."

CHAPTER THIRTY-SEVEN

One Thing at a Time

In bed, Nessa lay atop her buffalo robe, waiting for sleep, Green curled at her side. Both windows were open to a slight breeze that was beginning to stir the air of her hot upstairs room. She pulled her quilt alongside her to use as a pillow.

Holding a corner to her cheek, she pictured her mother in a pretty dress and someone — possibly an auntie? — who had saved the dress for her. Then she ran her fingers over the white rose sewn from a christening gown.

Did this mean one of the babies died? The only thing her father noted in his Bible was ". . . but the twins live."

So many questions ran through Nessa's mind. How did she get from Wisconsin to Missouri? Why was she sent to an orphanage instead of to grandparents or a neighbor? If the twins were alive, they'd be about ten years old now. Where were they?

Maybe more answers lay buried in her trunk, but she'd already taken everything out at least twice. So far, very little made sense to her. She needed time to carefully study each item. When Nessa at last grew sleepy, a prayer was in her heart.

Thank You, Lord, for helping me find Mama and Papa . . . and if I have brothers or sisters, please help me find them, too. . . .

After morning chores, Nessa walked to the bookstore. It was actually a square canvas tent with a wooden sign propped against one of its poles: PRAIRIE RIVER BOOKS. There were just two shelves, but they were full of dime stories, old issues of *Harper's Weekly Magazine* for fifteen cents, and novels.

She was looking through a book called *Letter-Writer*, when Laura walked in. She wore a brown dress buttoned up to her chin with a lace collar and a brown hat trimmed in blue.

"Oh, Nessa, it's so nice to see you," she said, reaching out a gloved hand. "What have you got there?"

"This? *A Guide to All Kinds of Correspondence.* I want to learn how to write a proper letter." Nessa didn't mention that she was going to start writing to some of the addresses she found on envelopes in her trunk or that she was seeking employment in Missouri. "And you?" she asked.

"Well," said Laura, "Fanny Jo's feeling blue so I thought something to read would lift her spirits."

Nessa remembered the conversation she overheard at the seamstress's shop and wished Laura would tell her more. When no explanation came about *why* her sister was feeling blue, Nessa said, "I know! Once you've picked a book, let's go to Filmore's and buy Fanny Jo a ribbon she can use for a bookmark. I have some pennies left."

Laura's face brightened. She took two dollars from her handbag and paid for *Vanity Fair: A Novel Without a Hero, Illustrated.* "It's expensive," she said, "but I couldn't find a copy in the library. My sister will love this, especially with all these pictures."

When they reached Mr. Filmore's store, Ivy was arranging spools of colored thread inside a glass case.

"Oh, hello!" she said. "I was hoping you'd come by."

Nessa felt happy that Ivy wanted to see her until she realized that Ivy wasn't talking to *her*. She had taken Laura by the elbow and was showing her a display of silver hat pins.

"Remember the ones we were talking about last time?" Ivy asked.

"Why, yes!" said Laura. "Do they have the pearl tips? I love those."

"Me too. And, also . . ."

Nessa felt as if her ears were ringing. Laura and Ivy were talking to each other as if they were old friends! How could that have happened? *I've known Laura the longest; after all, we came out on the stage together.*

Then she remembered. Except for confiding in Mrs. Lockett, Nessa had carefully avoided revealing anything personal to anyone. She kept herself locked away, like the things in her trunk. How would friends ever learn about her if they couldn't see what was inside?

". . . so won't you come to tea again?" Laura was asking

Ivy. "How does three this afternoon sound? It would truly cheer my sister. She still laughs about your first visit when . . ." She stopped herself and looked at Nessa.

"Oh, I'm sorry. Would you like to come, too, Nessa? Please do."

Nessa looked down at her scuffed shoes and thought how nice it would be to sit by herself at the creek, her feet in the cool water. Then she could return to her room and explore her trunk.

But in a moment of clarity, she realized there was something more important.

"Yes," she answered. "Actually, I'd love to come. Thank you."

CHAPTER THIRTY-EIGHT

Daisies

"Yoo-hoo, everyone, here's more," called Fanny Jo as she walked from the back porch into the house, a basket of berries on her arm. Behind her came Laura, carrying two full pails. Their swept-up hair held bits of twigs and leaves. Their cheeks glowed with color. Both wore long, white aprons, now speckled violet from berry juice.

It was jam day. Mrs. Lockett's kitchen was steaming hot from kettles boiling on her stove. The sweet aroma of fruit filled the air.

All morning the sisters had been at the creek with Ivy, picking from the berry thickets. Nessa was hurt they hadn't invited her to join them. At their tea the other day, she envied the casual way Ivy and the sisters had laughed together and shared personal stories. They'd been quite friendly to Nessa, so in her heart she was sure they weren't purposely leaving her out. Most likely they were used to doing things without her. She just wished she knew how to blend into their threesome.

Nessa instead took the younger girls — Minnie, Augusta, and Lucy — to gather from bushes that rimmed the boardinghouse garden. Though their arms were scratched, and their fingers and lips were stained from tastings, the little girls chattered happily, sticking out their purple tongues at one another.

Mrs. Lockett flustered about, arranging jars on the long oak table and the sink. "Dear me," she said, "we're running low on sugar. Nessa, honey, would you mind going to the store for me? I think five pounds'll do for now. Mr. Filmore is still waiting on a supply wagon, so go to Mr. Applewood. Just have him put it on my account."

Nessa hung up her apron and grabbed an empty basket for her walk to town. She hoped no one noticed her lack of cheer. She was still disappointed about being left out of Ivy's easy friendship with the sisters, and now the last thing she felt like doing on this hot August morning was facing the difficult Applewoods. What if they wouldn't sell her sugar on Mrs. Lockett's account? What if they again shamed her in front of strangers?

Walking toward the sutler's, Nessa wished for the day when these dusty paths would have wooden sidewalks like a real town. As she kicked a dirt clod, she remembered last evening in her room as she flipped through her father's Bible. She had not been praying or looking for anything in particular when her eyes fell on a passage in the sixth chapter of Luke. It was underlined in blue ink, a verse Miss Eva had helped her memorize when she was younger.

. . . love your enemies, do good to them which hate you, bless them that curse you, and pray for them which despitefully use you . . . and as ye would that men should do to you, do ye also to them likewise.

Nessa wondered what events in her father's life had caused him to mark these words of Jesus and write AMEN! in the margin. Right away, Mr. and Mrs. Applewood came to mind. It was hard for her to pray for them — in fact, every time she tried, she instead found herself complaining to God and listing the many ways they'd hurt her. And what did it mean to bless someone? To what purpose and why bother?

The water trough at the livery stable was filled to its brim. Green stood on her hind legs, her front paws on the wooden edge, to take a drink. Nearby in the dirt was a patch of yellow daisies. Nessa remembered how good she felt when Albert once had surprised her with a flower for no particular reason. Without thinking enough to talk herself out of it, she picked a handful, put them in her basket, then headed up for the store.

I don't feel like doing anything nice for them, she thought, *but since Jesus said to, I will . . . but that's the only reason. Maybe their insults won't bother me today.*

Two customers were in the store, looking at bolts of cloth when Nessa walked in. The bell jingling against the door drew Mr. Applewood's attention. Green's paws clicked along the wood floor as she followed Nessa.

"What is it this time?" he asked.

"Five pounds of sugar, please. We're making jam and

Mrs. Lockett is almost out." Nessa set her basket on the counter, relieved he hadn't said anything mean about her puppy.

She could see his wife in the back room at a desk, writing in a ledger.

While Mr. Applewood scooped sugar from a barrel and weighed it on a scale, Nessa untied a blue ribbon from one of her braids, then wrapped it around the stems of the daisies.

"These are for the missus," Nessa said, holding up the bouquet. She bit her lip, anticipating his reply.

"Give 'em to her yourself," he said. Turning toward the other room he called, "Someone's here to see you." He didn't use either of their names.

A chair scraped against the floor as the woman left her desk and came up front. Her husband busied himself by pouring sugar from the scale into a small burlap sack.

"What d'you want?" asked Mrs. Applewood.

"These are for you," Nessa said. She tried to be cheerful, but nearly lost heart by the way the woman stared at her, her pinched mouth unsmiling.

A long moment passed — so long, the clock struck noon and chimed twelve times, before she reached over the counter and accepted the flowers from Nessa.

"What d'you want for 'em?"

"Oh, nothing at all," she answered. "I was walking here and saw them and thought of you." It was the truth. Nessa didn't want to explain the argument she had had with herself about should-she-shouldn't-she, or that the idea came from Jesus. She was afraid the woman would laugh at her.

Mrs. Applewood studied the bouquet. "I always did like daisies," she said, then returned to her desk without another word.

Nessa put the sack of sugar in her basket and carried it home to the boardinghouse. For a while, she felt crushed that Mrs. Applewood didn't thank her, but that low feeling was being replaced by a tiny spot of joy. She couldn't understand why she felt so good.

CHAPTER THIRTY-NINE

The Artist

On jam day, the sisters stayed to help Mrs. Lockett with supper because special guests were coming. Nessa remembered seeing a crisply starched apron in her trunk, under the Bible.

"Be right back," she called as she ran upstairs two steps at a time. When she flung open the lid, the scent of new memories touched her, but instead of feeling grief she felt hopeful.

The apron was simple, white with red embroidered around the neckline. She smiled at the intitials, CCC, stitched at the hem. Claire Christine Clemens . . . *Mama.* As she tied the thick bow behind her waist, she noticed in the trunk something she saw last time: a tiny wooden box, the size of her hand. She had not yet opened it.

Nessa sat on her bed and took a deep breath. *May as well,* she thought, then counting to three in her head, lifted the lid. Inside was a thin leather collar with a silver bell, and a folded piece of parchment. Carefully, she uncreased the paper. On it was a drawing of a raccoon holding a strawberry with its front paws. Nessa sniffed the collar. That was it. The familiar smell from her buffalo robe and her puppy was a memory of her pet raccoon. She looked at the picture again.

Written in beautiful penmanship were the words "Buddy's favorite breakfast," followed by the initials, CCC.

Nessa closed her eyes. She could see her mother sitting by a window with paper in her lap, drawing.

Thank You, Jesus . . . thank You for giving me a good memory. . . . Buddy . . . and for reminding me Mama was an artist. . . .

She pressed the collar to her heart, returned it to its box, then raced downstairs.

As the sun slipped toward the horizon, Rolly and Reverend Ames set up tables in the yard. Stools, benches, and chairs were brought out. The air was hot, but soon it would be dusk and they could eat by lantern light. Even with the wind, it was usually cooler after sunset.

Mrs. Lockett and the sisters carried platters covered with cloth. Nessa arranged forks and knives and plates. Minnie drew water from the river to fill the pitchers.

All was ready when a wagon appeared, rattling up from the creekside trail. Minnie was beside herself with excitement. She loved it when her mother invited friends to supper.

"It's different," she explained to Nessa. "Mama's payin' guests leave after a couple days. But friends, well, we can see them again and again. That's why we call 'em 'special guests.'"

As Mrs. Bell stepped down from her wagon, she handed baby Oliver — now four months old — to Fanny Jo, who immediately cooed over him. Just then, Mr. Button arrived, carrying a pan of johnnycake he baked himself, and a moment later, Ivy with her father. They brought three raspberry pies, steam still rising from the poked crusts.

Ivy leaned close to Nessa. "I heard you like brown sugar, Nessa, so I put lots in."

Nessa beamed at Ivy's offer of friendship.

Reverend Ames had just finished saying grace when Nessa's puppy ran in front of them, dragging a roasted chicken. A moist trail led back to one of the tables where a platter lay upside down in the dirt.

Nessa held her breath, waiting for Mrs. Lockett's reaction. But Rolly and Minnie burst into such unrestrained laughter, their mother couldn't help herself. She laughed until she needed to wipe her eyes with the hem of her apron.

"Well, I'll be," said Reverend Ames. "That's the first time a dog ever beat *me* to the supper table."

The Bells were the last to wave good night to Mrs. Lockett. A full moon would guide them back to their homestead near the lower creek.

Nessa hung out the wet dishtowels and swept the kitchen floor before saying good night herself. She carried her candle upstairs with some stationery so she could write Albert and Miss Eva. Again, she would send along two dollars toward paying off her debt.

"I've found my family," would be her first sentence, one she had practiced in her mind for days.

She looked at the floor where her puppy slept. Green was on her back, wedged along a wall, her paws in the air. This always made Nessa laugh, to see her like this. She leaned over from her bed to rub the plump belly.

"How was your chicken dinner, you naughty girl?" The tail swept side to side. "Good night, Green." She petted her again, closed the trunk so she could use the top for a writing desk, then began her letters.

Nessa had just used candle wax to seal the envelopes when Mrs. Lockett tapped on her door.

"Good night, dear, and thank you again for all your help today."

"Oh, wait, Mrs. Lockett, look at this." Nessa reached under her pillow for the picture of Buddy and showed it to her.

"I can't remember exactly what happened to our little raccoon," Nessa said, "but I think we let him go back into the woods. There was a lake near a forest; Papa had a canoe . . ."

Mrs. Lockett said, "You remember all that?"

"Well," she said, "this helped." She lifted a leather folder from the side of her bed and opened the flap. It was filled with drawings done in ink; some were sketched in pencil.

Nessa carefully pulled out the top sheet of paper. It showed a two-story house at the edge of a lake, surrounded by pine trees. A short dock led to the beach and tied to it was a canoe.

"I was little when I last saw my parents," said Nessa, "but now with this picture, I remember our house clearly. I just wish I could see their faces. . . ."

"Do you think . . ."

". . . there're more drawings in the trunk?" Nessa took a deep breath. "Maybe. But some other day."

Mrs. Lockett patted her hand. "And we have lots of them ahead of us."

CHAPTER FORTY

Full Bloom

From the garden where the children were filling baskets with ripe squash and cucumbers, Nessa looked at the schoolhouse. A window reflected the afternoon sunlight as if it were a mirror. For miles in every direction the prairie spread like an ocean, wind rippling over the surface of its golden grass. The sky was blue with a row of clouds building in the distance. Thunder hinted of rain.

In her letter to Albert, Nessa struggled to find words to describe the beauty and her affection for her new home and its people.

"I hope you'll come visit me and see for yourself," she wrote. "Mr. Button could use some help with his newspaper."

The shriek of children laughing reminded her of her task. She walked among the tall hollyhocks and sunflowers until she found a plump green watermelon. She hefted it into her arms, then carried it through a patch of poppies, daisies, and lavender, down the path to the creek. Lining this path were assorted vines and flowers, sprouted these past weeks from the children's pails spilling over.

At the creek, Nessa lowered the watermelon into a shallow pool. Before heading back to town, she would bring everyone here to cool off and, with a stone, break open the melon. Then after they'd eaten and rinsed off their hands, Rolly was going to drive them in his wagon to the cemetery. So far this summer they had managed to water Peter's tree every day. The children wanted it to become the biggest and proudest one in town. Nessa wanted that, too.

During supper, Nessa ate only a few bites of potato. Her stomach was nervous. In an hour the school committee was going to meet, and she wanted to be there to properly present herself.

During the last few days, she had carefully gathered her thoughts. Life was full of risks, she realized, whether she stayed here or returned to Missouri. Nessa had grown to love the Locketts and the life they'd opened up to her. She loved the wild beauty of the prairie. The bounty of the garden she and the children created together renewed her faith in herself. She *was* a good teacher who cared deeply for her students. And remembering her words to Albert — *my new home* — Nessa realized her heart lay in Prairie River.

In her trunk, she had found a small hatbox and in it a pair of white lace gloves with a hat that must have belonged to her mother. It was straw with a blue velvet ribbon around the crown and a stylish brim that curved downward over her cheeks.

I'm just fourteen, thought Nessa, *but I can still dress like a lady.*

While she brushed her hair into a fresh braid, she imagined her mother wore this, sitting by her father in church. She looked in the small mirror over her bureau, adjusted her hat, then pinched her cheeks for color. She felt like a real schoolteacher.

As she walked to the Applewoods', she knew there would be people who didn't like her, people who wanted her to leave town.

I can only try, she thought, practicing in her mind what she would say:

"Good evening, everyone. . . . I'm Vanessa Ann Clemens and I would like very much to be Prairie River's teacher next term."

About the Author

Kristiana Gregory was born in Los Angeles, California. She has always wanted to be a writer and received her first rejection letter (for a poem) at age eleven. After graduating from high school, she began taking a variety of college courses and jobs, including positions as a daily news reporter and a book reviewer for the *Los Angeles Times*, that helped prepare her for her writing career. Her first book, *Jenny of the Tetons*, won the Golden Kite Award for fiction. She has contributed numerous titles to Scholastic's Dear America and Royal Diaries series. Kristiana has also written several books about the Old West and California history. *Earthquake at Dawn*, her book about the 1906 San Francisco earthquake, won the 1993 California Book Award for best juvenile fiction.

Married for twenty years, she lives in Boise, Idaho, with her husband, their two teenage sons, and two golden retrievers.